Paul Stewart is the very funny, very talented author of more than twenty books for children, including *The Edge Chronicles*, a collaboration with Chris Riddell.

Chris Riddell is a well-known illustrator and political cartoonist. His work appears in the *Observer* and the *New Statesman*. He has illustrated many picture books and novels for young readers, including *Pirate Diary* by Richard Platt, which won the 2001 Kate Greenaway Medal.

Both live in Brighton, where they created the Blobheads together.

'Richly inventive and lucidly written' *TES*

Also by Paul Stewart and Chris Riddell:

Muddle Earth

The *Rabbit and Hedgehog* books:
A Little Bit of Winter
The Birthday Presents
Rabbit's Wish
What Do You Remember?

The Edge Chronicles:
Beyond The Deepwoods
Stormchaser
Midnight Over Sanctaphrax
The Curse of the Gloamglozer

PAUL STEWART
& CHRIS RIDDELL

MACMILLAN CHILDREN'S BOOKS

Invasion of the Blobs, Talking Toasters, School Stinks! and *Beware of the Babysitter*
first published individually 2000 by Macmillan Children's Books

This edition published 2003 Macmillan Children's Books
a division of Macmillan Publishers Limited
20 New Wharf Road, London N1 9RR
Basingstoke and Oxford
www.panmacmillan.com

Associated companies throughout the world

ISBN 0 330 41353 8

1 3 5 7 9 8 6 4 2

A CIP catalogue record for this book is available from
the British Library.

Typeset by SX Composing DTP, Rayleigh, Essex
Printed and bound in Great Britain by Mackays of Chatham plc, Kent

Invasion of the Blobs

P. S. For Joseph and Anna
C. R. For William

Chapter One

Billy Barnes stood in the bathroom brushing his teeth. His dad's Toffee and Avocado Surprise was clamped to the inside of his mouth like cement. It would not budge. Billy put his toothbrush down and tried to dislodge the stuff with his fingernails.

"I wish we could just have ice cream for afters, like everybody else," he muttered. But Billy knew that, like wishing it could be Christmas every day, this would never happen.

His mum's executive career left her with far too little time to cook. While his dad's job – as house-husband and main carer of Billy and Silas – left him with far too much. And this week he had completed his evening class in Creative Cookery (Advanced).

Today's menu had been Curried Strawberry Soup, then Liver and Peach Roulade, followed by the gluey pudding.

"Unnkh!" Billy grunted as a toffee impression of his top teeth clunked down into the sink.

"Bang!" came a noise from behind him.

Billy spun round, heart thumping. The noise had come from the toilet.

"The seat must have dropped down," he told himself. "That's all."

He turned back and prodded inside his mouth again. A second lump of toffee dropped into the sink. Billy was just checking that none of his teeth had fallen out when he noticed a movement in the mirror.

Billy froze. It was the toilet again. Slowly but surely, the cover and the seat were rising up. Then, as he stared open-mouthed, something appeared in the gap. Something purple and red. Something blobby. Something horribly like his dad's Pickled Grape Jelly with Raspberry Coulis – except for one thing.

It had eyes!

"Waaah!" Billy screamed.

The purple and red thing disappeared and the toilet seat banged shut. There was a muffled cry of anger followed by splashing and spluttering.

Billy turned and stared at the toilet in horror.

He leapt forwards, seized the toilet handle and pressed it down. At first there was the familiar whoosh of the toilet flushing. Then everything went horribly wrong.

The toilet began glugging and gurgling, and water gushed out from beneath the seat.

"Oh, no!" Billy gasped. The water poured down onto the floor and sloshed over the tiles.

All at once, the toilet cover flew up and out popped the thing. The thing with the blobby head and the beady eyes. The thing that Billy hoped he had only imagined.

"Waaah!" he screamed again.

The thing climbed onto the toilet rim and looked around. From behind it, there came a squelchy PLOP! and a second thing popped up, followed almost at once by a third.

"Waaah!" screamed Billy for the third time.

The first thing fixed him with its two beady eyes. *"Waaaah!"* it screeched. The other two joined in. *"Waaaah! Waaaah!"* they bellowed, grinning and nodding as they did so.

Terrified, Billy stepped back. "Wha' . . . wha' . . . wha' . . ." he said. He'd *wanted* to ask who they were, why they were there and what they were doing in his toilet. But the words wouldn't come.

"Wha'. Wha'. Wha'," the three things repeated cheerfully.

Then the third thing slipped. It grabbed the second thing, which grabbed the first thing, which lost its

balance, and all three of them toppled from the toilet and landed – with a CRASH! – on the floor.

If he hadn't been so frightened, Billy might have laughed. The three things climbed to their feet – all nine of them – and smoothed their belted tunics down with long tentacle-arms.

"I thought you said they could talk!" the first one said to the third.

"Yes," said the second angrily. "*Waaaah, waaaah, wha', wha'*! This language is unknown to me."

"It's an Earthling greeting," said the third knowingly. "I thought everyone knew that!"

As one, they turned to Billy. The purple and red blobs on their heads throbbed in unison.

"Can – you – speak?" they asked together; very slowly, very clearly.

"Y-y-y . . ." Billy stammered.

"You see," said the first thing triumphantly. "Not a word."

"Yes," Billy blurted out. "I can speak."

Surprised, all three things leaped backwards and trilled with delight.

"Greetings, Earth boy," said the first, raising a tentacle in salute. "We are the Blobheads of Blob. Second, third and . . . thirty-eighth wonders of the cosmos. My name is Kerek. This is Zerek. And that," he said with an airy wave of a tentacle, "is Derek."

"Greetings," said Zerek as he looked beneath the bathmat. "We seek the High Emperor of the Universe."

"We come in pieces," said Derek.

"We come in *peace*," said Kerek irritably.

Billy swallowed nervously. "G-good,"

he said. "But I don't think you'll find the High Emperor of the Universe here," he added.

The first Blobhead frowned. "This is the Barnes household, number 32 Beech Avenue, Winton Bassett, Earth, is it not?"

"Yes," said Billy uncertainly. "And I am Billy. But . . ." He'd been warned about talking to strangers – and they didn't come much stranger than the three Blobheads.

"Then this is the place," said Kerek. "The Great Computer is never wrong."

"The Great Computer?" said Billy.

Kerek nodded. "It—"

Before he could explain, Billy heard his dad calling from the hall. "Are you going to be much longer in there?"

"Nearly ready," Billy called back as Zerek and Derek trotted off to explore

9

. . . and experiment! They turned the taps full on, they squeezed tubes, they squirted aerosols . . .

"Who's that?" asked Kerek.

"My dad," Billy whispered.

Zerek replaced the toilet brush he had been sniffing and looked up. "One half of the production team which made him," he explained to Kerek and Derek.

"The female half," said Derek, who was busy nibbling the towels.

Billy smiled. "Actually it's— Oh, what!" he exclaimed as he noticed the state of the bathroom.

The basin was overflowing with bubbly water; there was toothpaste on the walls and hair gel in the bath; the forbidden medicine cabinet was open and empty, its contents floating in the growing pool of water on the floor.

"Stop it!" he yelled at the rummaging Blobheads. He turned off the taps, grabbed one of the shredded towels and began mopping up the sticky mess. "And don't just stand there!" he said. "Help me!"

"Billy?" His father was knocking at the bathroom door. "What are you up to?"

Billy gulped. "Nothing, Dad."

"Open the door, then," he said. "It's time for Silas's bath."

"Yes . . . I . . . Just coming . . ." He turned to the Blobheads. "What about you?" he whispered.

"Don't worry about us," Kerek whispered back. "Hyper-intelligent beings like us know how to blend in."

"We are masters of disguise," said Zerek.

"Morphtastic!" said Derek.

"Billy!" shouted his dad. "Open this door at once."

Billy had no choice. He slopped his way over to the door and slid the bolt across. His dad peered in.

"There's been a slight accident," he confessed. "There was this—"

"Waaaah!" screamed his dad. "I can see it!"

Billy spun round. Totally ignoring

the armchair and ironing board which had suddenly appeared in the middle of the floor, Mr Barnes stared at the giant purple and red cockroach in the bath. It was a monster, the size of a large dog. Its feelers trembled. "Waaaah!" it shrieked.

"*Waaaah!*" screamed Billy's dad even louder. He backed out of the room. "Billy get out of there," he said.

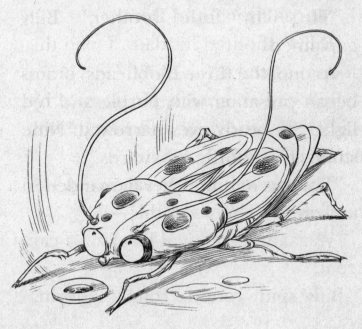

He turned and raced down the stairs. "I'll call the pest control people. The zoo. The police . . ."

Billy turned back, hands on hips. "Masters of disguise!" he said. "Morphtastic! Huh!"

The armchair, the ironing board and the cockroach became Kerek, Zerek and Derek again.

"Who is this *Silas*?" asked Kerek.

"He's my little brother," Billy explained.

As one, the three Blobheads' brains began pulsating with purple and red light. Six beady eyes narrowed. Nine stubby feet shuffled forwards.

"Take us to him," they demanded in unison.

Chapter Two

Silas was sitting in his cot banging on a small drum with his teddy. He looked up and gurgled.

Billy snorted. "Blobheads, Silas. Silas, Blobheads."

"Bobbolblobbolbobbobblob . . ." said Silas.

To Billy's surprise, instead of laughing, the three Blobheads fell on their knees.

"Oh, Most High Emperor of the Universe," said Kerek. "It is you."

"Bollobol," Silas giggled.

"Many *many* light-years," replied Zerek, nodding. "We used the alpha-gamma space–time wormhole."

"Blobbolobbolob."

"The *only* way to travel," said Derek.

Billy shook his head in amazement. "Are you telling me you can understand what he's saying?"

"The Most High Emperor's words are wise indeed," said Kerek.

Zerek reached inside the cot, wrapped his tentacles around Silas and pulled him out. "Right," he said, looking round furtively. "Let's be off, before someone else comes."

"Off?" Billy cried out. "What do you mean? And where are you going with my brother?"

Silas could certainly be a pain –

particularly since they shared a room –
but seeing him being carried off by
the Blobheads brought out all sorts of
feelings Billy didn't even know he had.
"Put him down!" he roared.

"Yes, put him down," said Kerek.
"The wormhole portal isn't due back
for another eleven minutes and eight
seconds."

"But . . . this is crazy," said Billy.
"Look at him. He can't possibly be the
Most High anything of anywhere. He
isn't even a year old yet."

"Or, to put it another way," said
Kerek, "fifty dicrons old – as predicted
in the *Book of Krud*. For, as it was
written, 'You will know him by these
signs. His nose will ooze greenness. He
will smell of sour earth. A creature
with unusually large ears will cover his
chest.'"

"But that's just snot and poo," said Billy.

Zerek looked round anxiously. "Where?" he said.

"He's got a bit of a cold," Billy explained. "And his nappy needs changing."

"And the creature?" Kerek demanded.

"It's Randy Rat!" said Billy. "A cartoon character . . ."

"Blobbollobol," said Silas, and pointed at the rat on his T-shirt proudly.

"You see!" said Kerek triumphantly.

But Billy didn't see. "He's my brother, and he belongs here."

"Wrong!" said Kerek. "He is the Most High Emperor of the Universe and he belongs with us, on Blob."

"It's the only way we can keep him

safe," said Zerek, and shuddered.

"Safe from the wicked Followers of Sandra," said Derek.

"Sandra?" Billy snorted.

"You may well scoff," said Kerek, "but the Followers of Sandra are dangerous. They would stop at nothing to take the Most High Emperor for their own. And if *that* happened . . ."

All three Blobheads quivered from head to foot with a sound like jelly sloshing in a bucket.

"Who is this Sandra?" said Billy.

"Not *who*," said Kerek, "but *what*, for Sandra is a—"

"Enough of this," said Zerek, looking around nervously. "We really should be getting back to that wet room. We don't want to miss the return of the wormhole."

He picked up Silas again.

Billy raced across the room, grabbed his brother's legs and pulled. "Let him go!" he shouted.

Zerek wrapped his tentacles around Silas's chest and pulled back. "*You* let him go!"

"No, *you* let him go!"

"No, YOU let him go!"

"You can both let him go!" Kerek instructed. "How dare you treat the Most High Emperor of the Universe in such a manner!"

Silas giggled happily as Zerek and Billy lowered him gently to the carpet. "Bloboblob," he said.

Derek stepped forwards. "We have a problem," he said. "*We* need to take the Most High Emperor to the safety of Blob. *Billy*, here, wishes him to stay."

"Mum and Dad would blame me if he disappeared," he said. "I know they would."

"Precisely," said Derek. "So we must ensure that he doesn't disappear." He unclipped a small black box – one of many – from his belt and aimed it at Silas.

"Hey!" Billy cried in alarm. "What are you doing?"

"Solving our problem," said Derek. He tapped the box. "With my Mega-nostic Multi-Scan Gizmo. Just lock on the coordinates. And . . . pasta!"

The box emitted a blinding flash. Billy screwed his eyes shut. When he opened them again he couldn't believe what he saw. Where one snotty, smelly Silas had been sitting, now there were two.

"There!" said Derek. "Now every-one's happy. We'll take the original and you can keep the copy."

"No one will ever know the differ-ence," said Kerek.

"And it's even got a clean nappy on," said Zerek hurriedly. "Now can we *please* depart, before—"

The box flashed a second time. Suddenly there were three Silases.

Again, and there were four.

Five. Six. Seven.

"Turn that thing off!" roared Kerek.

"I can't," said Derek, stabbing repeatedly at the box with his tentacle. "It's stuck!"

"That's all we need!" said Zerek dismally as a thirteenth Silas joined the rest. "And how are we supposed to tell which one is the *real* Most High Emperor of the Universe."

"Easy," said Kerek. "We sniff him out!"

Down in the hall, Billy's dad was having problems of his own. No one he called was impressed with his story of the giant cockroach. Not the pest control people. Not the zoo. And certainly not the police. He was calling the fire brigade when Mrs Barnes swept in through the front door.

"Meetings, meetings," she said, and blew her husband a kiss. "What's your day been like?"

Mr Barnes winced. "Hello?" he said. "Yes. I want to report a giant cockroach. It . . . Pardon? No, it's *not* on fire . . . What? Because I thought you could use your hoses to keep it at bay. I . . . Yes, just the one. But you

don't understand. It's colossal. The size of a pony—" The line went dead. ". . . at least," said Mr Barnes quietly. He turned to his wife. "She hung up," he said. "They all do."

"I'm not surprised," said Mrs Barnes. "A cockroach the size of a pony!" Her eyes narrowed. "What have you been cooking today?"

"Liver and Peach Roulade," said Mr Barnes proudly.

"Liver and . . . Oh, good grief!" Mrs Barnes exclaimed. "Are the children all right? Where are they anyway? Has Billy done his homework? Has Silas had his bath?"

"I . . . I . . ." Mr Barnes stammered.

"Oh, really!" Mrs Barnes snapped. "I get enough stress at work. The last thing I need when I get home is *more* stress! Giant cockroach indeed!"

"But there was," Mr Barnes said weakly.

Tutting impatiently, Mrs Barnes set off up the stairs. "Bil-ly! Si-las!" she called. "Mummy's home!"

The bedroom was overflowing with Silases by the time Derek finally managed to switch the machine off. Forty-seven in all there were – laughing, crying, crawling and dribbling, toddling and falling down. In amongst them were Kerek, Zerek and Derek – lifting, sniffing and replacing the babies, one after the other.

"He must be here somewhere!" said Kerek.

"But where?" said Zerek fretfully. "We'll never find him in time."

"Pfwoooarr!" said Derek, his blobby

head turning a shade of green. "I've found him."

At that moment, the door burst open. The Blobheads disguised themselves in an instant. Billy spun round.

"Mum!" he said.

"Billy!" she replied. "Silas." Her smile froze. "And Silas. And Silas. And Silas. And a watering can. And a toaster . . ." She closed her eyes and clutched her head. "Billy, love," she said. "Mum's had a very long day . . ." She opened her eyes again, and moaned.

The Silases were still everywhere. On the carpet. In the cot. And one in the arms of a gigantic fluffy blue kangaroo.

The room swam and Mrs Barnes fell to the floor in a dead faint. As she

landed, the watering can and toaster became Blobheads again. The fluffy blue kangaroo did not.

"Oh, Derek!" said Kerek and Zerek together.

"Sorry," said the kangaroo. It shrugged. "It happens."

"Yes, but always to you!" said Zerek furiously.

"All is not lost," said Derek. He stuffed Silas down inside his pouch and hopped towards the door. "Come on, you two," he said. "There isn't a moment to lose."

Chapter Three

Leaving his mum lying on the floor surrounded by the forty-six identical copies of Silas, Billy hurried after Zerek and Kerek and the fluffy blue kangaroo that was making off with his brother.

"Dad!" he yelled as he raced along the landing. "*Dad*!"

"Just a minute, Billy," he shouted back. "I'm on the phone . . . Hello? Is that the army?"

"But we haven't got a minute!" cried Billy. He raced to get to the bathroom door before the Blobheads could lock him out – and arrived just in time.

"Waaaah!" shrieked Zerek as the opening door propelled him across the slippery floor.

Kerek was looking down at a small black box of his own. "Ten seconds and counting," he said.

The fluffy blue kangaroo patted Silas down in his pouch and prepared to leap.

"Three . . . two . . . one . . ." said Kerek. "*Now!*"

The kangaroo leapt forwards into the toilet.

Billy gasped. He'd failed. The Blobheads were abducting his baby brother and there was nothing he could do to stop them.

"It's for the best," Kerek assured him.

"It's the only way," said Zerek.

"It's not here!" said the fluffy blue kangaroo.

"What?" screamed Kerek.

"The wormhole portal," said Derek. "It's not here."

"But it must be!" Zerek wailed. "How else are we going to get back?"

As Derek climbed out of the toilet bowl, Kerek inspected the screen on his small black box. "It makes no sense," he said. "The Great Computer stated that the wormhole would return to the same spot thirty minutes and nineteen seconds after—"

"No," said Zerek. "You're wrong. The confibulation matrix has quabbled, causing a tiny but significant difference in position. Five Earth metres to be precise. Which means . . ." He cocked his blobby head to one side. "Listen!"

From the other end of the landing, came a soft, swooshing *sucking* sound.

"That's *it*!" shouted Kerek. "To the bedroom at once!" And back they all ran.

"The size of an elephant, I tell you!" Billy heard his dad shouting down the phone. "Hello? Hello?"

They burst into the bedroom together: Kerek, Zerek, the fluffy blue kangaroo with Silas in its pouch, and Billy himself. Mrs Barnes, who was just coming round, raised her head, blinked twice, rolled her eyes and went out like a light once again.

"Look!" said Kerek, and pointed unnecessarily. They could all see the translucent tube swaying this way and that around the room, sucking copy

after copy of Silas in through its dark circular portal.

"It's already gone unstable," said Zerek nervously. "Four or five seconds more, and it'll be gone. Quick!" he screamed, and made a dash for the opening.

Unfortunately, Kerek and the kangaroo also had the same idea at exactly the same moment. The three of them – four, including Silas – ended up sprawled across the floor. Silas crawled out of the fluffy blue pouch.

"Blobberlobbolblob," he said, and pointed at the last of his twins as he too was sucked up inside the gleaming wormhole. Silas climbed to his feet and toddled after him.

"*No!*" bellowed Billy. He leaped forwards, grabbed Silas under the arms and pulled him away. Abruptly the wormhole quivered, faded and disappeared.

Silas was outraged. His face turned purple, his eyes screwed shut, his mouth snapped open and he screamed and screamed.

"See what you've done?" Kerek said to Billy. "The Most High Emperor of the Universe is displeased."

Billy looked down at the little ball of rage. "One day he'll thank me," he said.

"And us?" said Zerek. "What is to become of us?" He turned on Derek. "This is all your fault!" he said.

"Mine?" said Derek, shaking his fluffy blue kangaroo's head. "Why?"

Silas screamed all the louder.

"Because it's *always* your fault!" yelled Zerek.

"Now, now, fellow Blobheads," said Kerek. "Squabbling is pointless. Let us see what the Great Computer has to say . . ."

"Waaaah!" screeched Silas. "*Waaaah!*"

Billy looked down at his mum. The noise was waking her up. Her eyelids were flickering. "She's coming round!" he whispered urgently. "And Dad's coming!" he added as he heard the sound of heavy feet pounding up the stairs.

"What do we do? What do we do?" squealed Zerek, spinning round and round.

"In the wardrobe, all of you," said Billy, pulling the door open for them.

Kerek nodded. "You won't betray us, will you?" he asked as he climbed in.

"Of course not," said Billy.

"We have ways of dealing with traitors," said Derek threateningly – or rather, as threateningly as it is possible for a giant fluffy blue kangaroo to be. As Derek pulled the wardrobe door shut, the door opposite flew open. Mr Barnes burst in. He saw his wife lying on the floor.

"Alison!" he cried, and raced to her

side. "What happened?"

Mrs Barnes sat up and looked round groggily. "Babies," she said. "Everywhere. And a gigantic fluffy blue kangaroo . . ."

"Bet it wasn't as big as that cockroach," he said.

Silas stopped screaming. "Blob blob," he said, and crawled past his mum and dad.

"Pfwoooarr!" said Mrs Barnes.

"I was just about to change his nappy," said Mr Barnes.

"*Silas*!" Billy yelled when he realized where his brother was heading. Straight towards the wardrobe!

Hadn't the Blobheads warned Billy that they must not be betrayed? With his heart in his mouth, he jumped forwards and made a grab for his little brother. But too late. Silas's pudgy hands were already tugging at the wardrobe door.

The hinges creaked. The door swung slowly open. Billy stared into the darkness inside – and gasped.

Chapter Four

"'Ello! 'Ello! 'Ello!" came a voice, and a short, fat policeman stepped out of the wardrobe and crossed the room to Billy's parents. "I understand you've been having a spot of bother with a giant cockroach," he said.

"Y-yes, Officer," said Mr Barnes as he climbed to his feet. "That's right. I . . ."

Mrs Barnes stared at the ludicrously small helmet wobbling about on the top of the policeman's enormous, *blobby* head. Her eyes narrowed. "What were you doing in that cupboard?" she demanded.

"Looking for clues," said the policeman. "I can tell you now that the said bug is not, and never has been, hiding there."

"But—" Mrs Barnes began.

"Don't worry, madam," the policeman said. "I'll soon get to the bottom

of this."

And with that, he hurried from the bedroom. As he did so, the wardrobe door opened for a second time.

"We've had an emergency call about a giant cockroach," said a tall, thin firefighter, dressed in a garish uniform the exact same colour as Mr Barnes's Lime and Anchovy Compote.

"Th-that was me," said Mr Barnes. "And thank you for coming so promptly."

"All in a day's work," the firefighter said. He slammed the wardrobe door shut. "You may rest assured that I shall not leave this house until the afore-mentioned creepy-crawly creature has been located and disposed of."

And so saying, he too made a speedy exit from the bedroom. Mr Barnes smiled sheepishly. "Good to see they

took my calls so seriously," he said.

At that moment, a noisy kerfuffle exploded from inside the cupboard. Mrs Barnes turned to her husband.

"Who else did you call?" she asked weakly.

"I . . . errm . . . Oh dear," he said.

"Well?"

"The army," he admitted.

Mrs Barnes groaned. "So I suppose

that's a soldier," she said. The frantic banging and crashing grew louder. "Or soldiers. It sounds as though there's a whole regiment of them in there!"

All eyes fell on the cupboard.

"Let me out!" came a muffled cry.

Mr and Mrs Barnes crossed the room and began tugging at the wardrobe door. Billy watched nervously.

"Let me out!" the voice cried again.

Mr and Mrs Barnes tugged at the door all the more desperately.

"Let me ou—!"

At that moment the catch clicked, the wardrobe door burst open and out sprung the gigantic fluffy blue kangaroo. Mr Barnes was sent flying. He landed on the floor with a loud CRASH! Mrs Barnes landed on top of him. And above them both towered

the fluffy blue kangaroo.

It looked down. "Sorry about that, madam, sir," it said. "I don't suppose either of you have seen a giant cockroach, have you?"

Mr Barnes shook his head. Mrs Barnes opened and shut her mouth, but could not speak.

"No matter," said the kangaroo as it bounded off towards the bedroom door. "You leave it all to me."

"You see!" screamed Mrs Barnes when it was gone. "I *told* you there was a kangaroo!"

Mr Barnes hugged his wife tightly. "I know you did. I . . ." He turned to Billy in desperation. "Do *you* know anything about all this?"

"Know about what?" he said, pretending to be puzzled.

"About *what?*" his dad exclaimed.

"About that gigantic fluffy blue kangaroo!" shrieked his mum.

Billy swallowed anxiously. He knew that no explanation would be good enough. "Gigantic fluffy blue kangaroo . . . ?" he said innocently. "What gigantic fluffy blue kangaroo?"

Chapter Five

"You both work too hard," said Billy sympathetically. "I'll tidy up in here and change Silas's nappy. You two go downstairs. Have a cup of Dad's dandelion and nettle tea. Put your feet up. Relax."

"Thank you, Billy," said his dad shakily. "I think we might just do that."

The moment Mr and Mrs Barnes had gone, Billy grabbed Silas and dashed back along the landing. "Where are you?" he hissed as loudly as he dared. "Kerek? Zerek?"

There was a noise from the bathroom. Billy went in. He saw the toilet seat slowly rising, and four beady eyes peek out.

"There you are!" he said. "Where's Derek?"

"Derek!" Kerek snorted. "Trust him to mess up. We'd have got away with it if it hadn't been for him."

"He's a disgrace!" said Zerek furiously.

"Never mind about all that," said Billy. "Where is he?"

At that moment, the shower curtain moved. Billy strode across the room and yanked it back.

"Waaah!" the kangaroo cried out – and abruptly turned back into a Blobhead. "*That* did the trick," he said. "I must have morphed because

you made me jump."

"Not as much as you made Mum and Dad jump," said Billy sternly.

Kerek frowned. "I can see we're going to have to be careful about our disguises."

"I had no idea humans were such timid creatures," Zerek sniffed.

"Grown-ups are," said Billy. "And if I know my mum and dad, it's going to take more than a cup of dandelion and nettle tea to calm them down."

"You're right," said Derek, stepping forwards. He handed Billy yet another of the small black boxes from his belt.

"What is it?" asked Billy suspiciously.

"It's a Positron Memory Massage Gizmo. One zap will remedy the situation," Kerek explained. "After all, if we're going to stay here . . ."

"You're staying?" Billy exclaimed.

"Until the wormhole returns," said Kerek.

"And when will that be?"

Kerek unclipped a small black box from his own belt and squinted down at the screen. "According to the Great Computer the next wormhole portal will be along again in another thirteen hours . . ."

He paused.

He frowned.

He rubbed a tentacle over his blobby head. "Or is that years?"

Zerek groaned. "Centuries, most like," he said. "Knowing *my* luck!"

Derek shuffled forwards and tickled Silas under the chin. "Perhaps it was

meant to be," he said. "After all, someone has to protect the Most High Emperor from the evil Followers of Sandra. It might as well be us."

Having tidied the room and changed Silas, as promised, Billy went downstairs. He found his parents sitting at the table in the kitchen. They looked awful.

His dad was hunched over with his head in his hands, his mum was staring unblinkingly at the wall. Before them, stood two steaming mugs of dandelion and nettle tea – untouched.

Billy looked down at the Positron Memory Massage Gizmo. "This had better work," he muttered. He took aim and fired. A dazzling bolt of light flew out across the room, swirled around his parents for a second – and disappeared.

Mrs Barnes looked up. "Fluffy blue kangaroo!" She smiled. "It's work. I've been under far too much stress recently."

"Of course you have," said Mr Barnes. "You need a break. We both do." He chuckled. "Giant cockroach indeed! It *must* have been something I ate!"

Billy sighed with relief. His parents were acting as though nothing had happened. At last the Blobheads had managed to come up with something that actually worked!

"All right, Mum, Dad?" he said brightly.

"Fine, thanks, Billy," said his dad as he rose several inches off his chair into the air. "I'm feeling *wonderful*."

Billy let out a soft, miserable groan. He might have known that there would be a hitch to the Blobhead's gizmo!

"Without a single care in the world," said his mum as she too floated dreamily up from the table.

"Good," said Billy nervously. "I . . . I'll just go and get Silas."

And with that he raced off to ask the Blobheads whether there was some little black box or other on their belts which would bring his parents back down to earth again.

"Oh, the side effects won't last long," Kerek assured him as roars of laughter and squeals of delight floated up from the kitchen.

Zerek glanced over at the bedroom clock. "In fact—"

At that moment, there was a loud

crash, followed by another. Mr and Mrs Barnes had come down at last – and with a bang!

Billy winced. "Uh-oh!" he said. "Is there anything you can do about a pair of badly bruised bottoms?"

"Of course!" said Kerek. "For we are the Blobheads of Blob. Second, third and . . ." he glanced at Derek, "ninety-third wonders of the cosmos. There is *nothing* we cannot do!"

Meanwhile, far, far away on the other side of the universe, in the outer reaches of the Spider Galaxy, the planet Blob circled its purple and red sun. It was a typical day. The sky was green. The air was stale. The clouds on the horizon suggested a slime-storm was imminent.

And at number 76, The Mouldings,

Vera and Zera – two elderly and, if truth be told, rather decrepit Blobheads – were wondering what on Blob they were going to do with the forty-six identical pink alien babies which had suddenly appeared in their bed chamber.

TALKING
TOASTERS

P. S. For Anna and Joseph
C. R. For Katy

Chapter One

"Blobheads!" Billy Barnes grumbled as he clattered about the kitchen. "They travel here from halfway across the universe. They've got cloning gadgets, memory gizmos – and brains the size of giant pumpkins. Yet what do they want to eat at six o'clock in the evening? Breakfast!"

He popped two slices of bread into the toaster.

"Breakfast for breakfast. Breakfast

for lunch. Breakfast for dinner, supper and tea . . ."

At that moment the kitchen door burst open.

"The High Emperor of the Universe needs his nappy changing," Kerek announced.

"Immediately!" said Zerek.

"But I'm getting your breakfast ready," said Billy.

"Never mind that," said Kerek. "Our mission is to protect and serve the High Emperor until we can return in triumph with him to Blob."

Billy rolled his eyes. "I keep telling you. He's my little brother and he's not going anywhere."

"We'll see about that," said Kerek. "In the meantime, his well-being is of maximum importance. You must change him at once. Where's the

nappy-rash cream?"

"I think Derek ate it last night for breakfast," said Billy.

"Typical!" Zerek exploded.

"Come on," said Kerek. "We're hyper-intelligent beings. Changing a nappy can't be *that* difficult. We'll do it ourselves."

Muttering to themselves, the two of them bustled out of the kitchen. Billy sighed. Living with three Blobheads wasn't easy. He opened the dishwasher and removed three clean plates.

"So, what did they want on their toast? Marmalade for Zerek. Peanut butter for Kerek. And what was it Derek asked for?"

Right on cue, the kitchen door burst open for a second time and in charged Derek. "How's that toast coming along?" he said. "I'm as hungry as a horse."

Billy smiled. "I could *eat* a horse," he corrected him.

"You could?" said Derek.

"No, not me," said Billy. "You."

Derek frowned. "You want *me* to eat a horse?" he said.

"No, I . . ."

"I don't think I'd like that," Derek said, his red and purple blobby head pulsating with disgust. "No, if it's all the same to you, I'll stick with the mashed baked beans and curry powder on toast," he said. "And don't forget the washing-up liquid – but just a dash!"

Billy nodded. Beans, curry and washing-up liquid. How could he have forgotten?

"So, what have you been doing?" Billy asked.

"This and that," said Derek vaguely. "Looking after the High Emperor. Chatting to Kevin . . ."

Billy laughed. "You spend more time with my pet hamster these days than I do . . ." He winced. "What's that smell?"

"Whoops! Pardon me," said Derek sheepishly. "That nappy-rash cream must have disagreed with me."

"No, not that," said Billy. "I . . . Burning! I can smell burning." He spun round. Bluey-grey smoke was coiling up from the toaster. "Oh no!" he yelled. "That's all I need!"

Billy dashed across the kitchen, lunged at the toaster and began stabbing at the eject button, to release the toast before the whole lot burst into flames. But the toast wouldn't budge. The smoke turned black.

"Stupid toaster!" Billy shouted angrily. "It's completely jammed. Stupid, stupid . . ."

"Hey, that's no way to talk to it!" said Derek.

"You what?" said Billy. "It's just a toaster!"

"Machines have feelings, too," said Derek. "Blobby Heavens, you wouldn't get far on Blob speaking to electrical appliances like that."

"Don't just stand there talking!" Billy bellowed. "*Do* something!"

The smoke thickened. Abruptly, the toaster disappeared from view. "Oh, blimey," said Billy, "now I can't even see enough to unplug it . . ."

Derek pushed Billy aside. "Leave it to me," he said.

This, Billy was only too happy to do. Standing back, he watched with growing fascination as the Blobhead shuffled forwards, reached up and began massaging his head.

"What are you . . .?" he began.

"Shhh!" said Derek. "I need to concentrate if the mental tentacle is to work."

Mental tentacle? thought Billy. *What on earth? . . .*

And then he saw, for, as Derek continued to rub the blobs on his head, one after the other, the largest blob of all began to fizz, pulse – and elongate.

Longer and longer it grew, brighter and brighter – coiling straight out of the top of Derek's head. Billy gasped. "What does it do?" he said.

"You'll see," said Derek. He leaned

forwards. The glowing tentacle swayed down through the air and attached itself to the side of the toaster with its suckers. For an instant, the toaster glowed and Billy thought he heard the chatter of a cross little voice. Then,

PING!

The familiar and oh-so-welcome sound of the toaster releasing the toast echoed round the smoky kitchen. Two squares of smoking charcoal flew up into the air. Derek caught them with a flourish.

"*Ta-da!*" he announced, and bowed.

"Brilliant!" said Billy. He frowned. "But I don't understand. How come it didn't let go of the toast before?"

"Coz you didn't ask nicely," came a sulky voice.

Billy stared at the toaster in surprise.

"In fact you didn't ask at all," it said.

"You just shouted. *And* called me stupid."

Billy's jaw dropped. He looked at the Blobhead for some kind of explanation.

"Crumpets, teacakes, great wads of granary bread," the toaster continued. "A *thank you* would be nice once in a while."

"I . . . I'm sorry," Billy stammered. "I didn't think . . ."

"That's just it," the toaster interrupted. "You didn't think." It sniffed. "But then none of you do. I'm taken for granted and that's the truth – I'd have walked out years ago if . . ." It paused. It turned pink. "If it hadn't been for Kettle."

"The kettle?" Billy exclaimed. He turned to Derek. "Can you do this to all the machines?" he asked.

73

"All the electrical ones," the Blob-head confirmed. The mental tentacle glowed and swayed. "Would you like to see?"

Billy grinned. "You bet!" he said.

Chapter Two

Five minutes later the kitchen was filled with the babble of voices – from the deep rumble of the oven to the cheeky squeakiness of the food-mixer. Billy listened in amazement.

"Kettle, my love," the toaster was calling out. "How I adore the curve of your handle, the gleam of your spout . . ."

"Oh, stop it!" the kettle called back. "I don't want to hear all this."

"You love someone else, don't you?" the toaster asked miserably.

"I do," the kettle whispered dreamily. "Microwave is *so* cool!"

"Kettle's in lo-ove!" the food-mixer cried out in a sing-song voice. "Kettle's in lo-ove!"

"Don't tease!" snapped the coffee grinder.

"Why? What are you going to do about it?" the food-mixer snapped back.

"You'll see!" the coffee grinder shouted.

"Yeah?" said the food-mixer. "You and whose army?"

"Oi! Stop picking fights," said the oven hotly.

"He started it!" the food-mixer protested.

"Why don't we *all* just quieten down," said the beige thing with five dials.

"Who asked *you*?" sneered the coffee grinder.

"Don't shout at me," the beige thing whimpered. "I'm just trying to be useful."

The dishwasher snorted. "If you want to be useful, you might try cleaning some of the dishes."

"That's not what I'm for . . ." the beige thing began.

"Well, what *are* you for?" demanded the dishwasher.

"I'm not sure," it admitted. "Something to do with waffles, I think. Or was it chapatis? Certainly not cleaning dishes!"

But the dishwasher was no longer listening. "Half the time I'm put on for no more than a tea-cup and a couple of spoons!" it complained. "And they *will* put that wretched wok in without rinsing it first. My drainage filters haven't been cleaned for weeks."

"Weeks?" exclaimed the oven. "You're lucky. And the food I'm expected to cook! Rhubarb and Bacon Cassoulet. Garlic Semolina. Toffee and Avocado Surprise. It's disgusting! And I have never, *ever* been cleaned!"

"Nor have we," shouted the fridge-freezer in unison.

"And Fridge is beginning to niff," Freezer added quietly.

"I heard that!" roared Fridge. "You could do with a good defrosting yourself."

The electric carving knife glinted menacingly. "Sometimes I get so angry!" it hissed menacingly.

Billy shivered uncomfortably. "Derek," he said. "This *is* OK, isn't it?" He thought of all the other times the Blobhead experiments had gone wrong. "I mean nothing horrible's going to happen, is it?"

"Of course not," said Derek. "And anyway, if it does, all you have to do is switch them off for a second. When they come back on again – Bob's your ankle – they'll be back to normal."

Billy nodded uncertainly.

"And another thing!" the dish-washer was shouting. "I'm always being put on at night."

"You and me both," said the kettle. "If I'm woken up to make one more cup of tea I'll go mad!"

"We're *always* working!" said the fridge-freezer.

"If you can call what *Pongo* does 'work'," said Freezer quietly.

"I *heard* that," cried Fridge.

"And what about me?" came a gloomy voice. The vacuum cleaner poked its nozzle round the cupboard door. "Nobody ever bothers to consider my feelings."

"That's just it," said the dishwasher. "No consideration. No gratitude. And I for one am not going to take it any more."

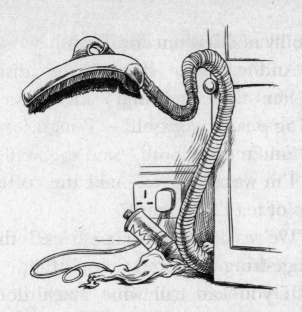

Billy shuffled about. "Perhaps we should turn them off now," he whispered to Derek.

"I want a good night's sleep!" cried the dishwasher.

"I want a good clean!" boomed the oven.

"I just want to be loved," sighed the toaster.

Billy swallowed nervously. They were all getting far, far too unruly –

like class 4T when Mr Trubshaw was out of the room.

"Shut up!" screeched Fridge.

"Shut up, yourself – Pongo," retorted Freezer.

"I'm warning you!" said the coffee grinder.

"Or was it Danish pastries?" the beige thing muttered thoughtfully.

Billy looked from one machine to the other, panic rising in his throat.

"Leave me alone!" screeched the kettle.

"Or I'll zap you from here to kingdom come!" shouted the microwave.

"And I'll smash your face in!" the toaster roared back.

"*FIGHT*! *FIGHT*!" the food-mixer announced excitedly.

"That's it," said Billy. He strode over

to the toaster and switched it off at the socket.

"I'll pulverize you!" the toaster roared, louder than ever. "I'll spiflicate you! I'll pull you to pieces!"

"Uh-oh," thought Billy. He turned anxiously to Derek.

"Try it again," the Blobhead advised him.

Billy did so. Off on. Off on. But it was no good. He tried unplugging it, but no matter how hard he tugged and pulled, the plug would not release its grip. The toaster would not be silenced.

And neither would any of the others.

Panic-stricken, Billy raced round the kitchen, flicking switches and tugging at plugs. But all in vain. Nothing worked. Nothing would undo the situation that Derek's mental tentacle had created. All round him, dials were whizzing, pingers pinging and flexes flexing. The air buzzed and rattled and throbbed.

"Pong-o! Pong-o!" Freezer taunted.

"I hate you!" Fridge said. "I wish you'd never been made."

"I can feel myself getting angrier and angrier," the electric carving knife whispered.

Billy trembled from head to foot. His mum and dad would be back from the shops at any moment.

"Why did I listen to you?" he said to Derek crossly. "I might have known that . . ."

Just then, in marched Kerek and Zerek. Zerek was holding Silas in his tentacle arms.

"These human nappies are *so*

84

primitive!" he complained.

"Never mind that!" Billy exclaimed. "LOOK!"

The two Blobheads stopped in the middle of the floor and stared round. Zerek placed Silas gently down and turned on Derek furiously.

"This is *your* doing, isn't it?" he roared. "You've been using your mental tentacle again."

"N . . . no, it isn't," Derek stuttered. "I haven't. I . . ."

"Don't lie to me," said Zerek. "Your central blob's still fizzing and pulsing. How many times must I tell you not to use your mental tentacle on your own. It's too dangerous."

"*You* do," said Derek sulkily.

"Yes, but *we* know how to," said Kerek. "*You* don't."

"But it's not right!" Derek protested loudly.

"*You're* not right," Zerek shouted back, and tapped his blobby head with his tentacled arms. "You're a planet short of a solar system . . ."

"Fellow Blobheads," Kerek shouted above the din. "This isn't helping. We're in an orange-alert situation. We must . . ." He paused. His purple and red head began to pulse furiously.

"What is it?" said Billy.

"They're back," said Kerek. "The two halves of the production team that made you."

"What?" said Billy.

"Your mum and dad!"

"Waaaah!" shrieked Zerek, and began dashing round in circles, blobs flashing. "Red alert! Red alert!"

Billy glanced up. The car was parked outside. His mum and dad were carrying bags of shopping up to the front door. Any second now the key would turn in the lock, the door would open . . .

"What do we do?" Zerek whimpered anxiously.

"There's only one thing for it," yelled Kerek. "Hide!"

And, as Billy watched, the three Blobheads transformed themselves.

Kerek became a red and purple play-table, Zerek, the chair to go with it.

"Coo," said Silas, as he toddled towards them and sat down. Then he gurgled with laughter and pointed.

Billy looked round at the giant fluffy blue kangaroo standing behind him. "Oh, Derek!" he shouted impatiently. "Must you *always* change into a kangaroo?"

"A mere technical hitch," said Derek. "I . . ."

"There's no time for this now," said Billy. "Hide yourself in the cupboard under the stairs."

As Derek hopped away, Billy frowned. The cacophony of voices was louder than ever. He put his hands on his hips and, in his best teacher's voice, cried out.

"SILENCE!"

Chapter Three

It was quiet in the kitchen. Too quiet. Billy crouched down beside Silas, who was crayoning at the table. Every tiny noise made him uneasy. Every squeak, every creak, every gurgle. It was as if he could *hear* the noisy rabble trying to remain still.

"Have you seen the Bolivian kumquats?" said Mr Barnes. "I need them for my Oyster Jambalaya."

"They're on top of the microwave," said Mrs Barnes as she unpacked the shopping. She paused. "What *is* Jambalaya?"

"A rice-dish from New Orleans," came the reply. "Though I'm going to try my own version."

Mrs Barnes raised her eyebrows. As house-husband, Mr Barnes took his cooking duties seriously – *too* seriously! She didn't have the heart to tell him she'd be more than happy with meat and two veg.

"Bother!" she heard him saying. "We're out of balsamic vinegar. I thought I had some in the fridge ..."

Mrs Barnes looked round. "I can't imagine how you know *what's* in that fridge. It's always so full."

"I know," said Mr Barnes. "I keep meaning to defrost it."

Mrs Barnes crossed the kitchen and looked inside. "*Pfwooar!*" she

exclaimed. "It could certainly do with a clean . . ."

"Pong-o!"

"I *heard* that!"

"Pardon?" said Mrs Barnes.

"What?" said Mr Barnes.

"I thought you said something."

Mr Barnes shook his head. "Not a word."

"Me neither," said Billy. "And I trust nobody else did," he added sternly.

"Funny, I could have *sworn* . . ." Mrs Barnes frowned. "Where do you want me to put the buckwheat? In the cupboard or . . . Whoops!"

She tripped. She tottered forwards. The packet of buckwheat fell to the floor, the plastic wrapper split and the grains spilled out all over the tiles like a swarm of tiny beetles. Mrs Barnes landed amongst them and looked round angrily.

"What on earth's the vacuum cleaner doing out?" she said. "I tripped over the wretched nozzle."

"Are you all right?" asked Mr Barnes. "I'll clean it all up."

Mrs Barnes rubbed her ankle tenderly and climbed to her feet.

"You could have said *sorry*," came an angry voice.

"I didn't drop it on purpose," she snapped.

"Pardon, dear?" said Mr Barnes.

"I didn't drop it on purpose," Mrs Barnes repeated.

"I never said you did."

"But . . ."

The vacuum cleaner droned into action. Mrs Barnes scratched her head, puzzled, and shrugged.

"I'll do that," she said, taking over from her husband. "You finish putting away."

It wasn't long before every single grain of buckwheat was gone. Mrs Barnes clicked the vacuum cleaner off and went to unplug it.

"A kindly word would be nice once in a while," complained a gloomy voice.

"Waaaaah!" screamed Mrs Barnes.

"What?" said Mr Barnes, alarmed.

"Voices!" Mrs Barnes said. "I keep hearing voices! Grumpy voices. Angry voices. Gloomy voices. I . . . I . . ."

Mr Barnes smiled and gave her a hug. "You work far too hard," he said. "Why don't you sit down? Have a nice cup of tea. I'll put the kettle on."

"That's *it*!" screeched a voice. "I warned you. One more cup of tea and I'll go mad, I said. And now I *am* mad."

Mr Barnes broke away from his wife and spun round.

"You heard that, didn't you?" Mrs Barnes shrieked. "*Now* do you believe me?"

"Yes, yes," said Mr Barnes. "I heard a voice but . . ." His eyes narrowed. "Billy?" he said.

Billy looked up to see his parents glaring at him.

"If this is one of your silly tricks," said his dad.

"What?" said Billy innocently.

"Those voices!" said his mum.

"Voices?" he said. "What voices? I don't know what you mean." Billy glared round the room furiously. "Everything is QUIET here!" he said. "QUIET! And that's the way it's going to stay. Nice and QUIET!"

Mrs Barnes looked at her husband and shrugged. It wasn't the first time Billy had been acting strange recently. "I . . . I could really do with that cup of tea," she said.

Mr Barnes nodded, reached out for the kettle and switched it on. Then he waited.

And waited and waited and waited . . .

"Blooming kettle," he muttered

impatiently. "We're going to have to get a new one. This one's hopeless."

"NO!" screeched the toaster, pinging and popping furiously. "Leave Kettle alone!"

Shocked, Mr Barnes stumbled back across the floor. First the kettle. Now the toaster.

The next moment, they were all at it.

"Toaster loves Kettle!" taunted the food-mixer.

"Oh, grow up!" the toaster fumed.

The food-mixer whirred menacingly. "Make me!" it shouted.

Mr and Mrs Barnes stared at Billy helplessly. "Wh . . . what's going on?" they both gasped in unison.

Billy went pale. What should he say? What *could* he say? Before he had a chance to say anything, the kettle piped up for him.

"We're fed up!" it said.

"You tell 'em!" yelled the microwave.

"We've been put upon for far too long," the kettle continued.

"Ooh, you are beautiful when you're angry," purred the toaster.

"And enough is enough!" the kettle shouted.

Others joined in – the microwave,

the washing machine, the fridge-freezer, the dishwasher – till the whole kitchen was shaking with years of pent-up anger and frustration.

Billy turned to Kerek and Zerek – but the red and purple table and chair had concerns of their own.

"High Emperor," the table whispered as Silas dropped to the floor and crawled away. "Come back!"

"This instant!" hissed the chair. "Billy, get the High Emperor."

But Billy couldn't move. It was as if he'd been rooted to the spot. The uproar grew louder.

"This is it!" the kettle screeched, furiously rattling its lid.

"The time has come!" bellowed the fridge-freezer as it banged its doors open and shut. It was trembling so hard that the food inside began tumbling from its shelves down onto the floor.

The electric carving knife began bouncing up and down. Its flex lashed. Its blade glinted. "Now I'm getting really, *really* angry," it snarled. "I could lose it at any moment . . ."

"Help!" Mr and Mrs Barnes cried out. "HELP!"

Chapter Four

Billy trembled from top to toe. Now he knew *just* how Mr Trubshaw must feel with 4T on a wet and windy Friday afternoon.

"Listen to me!" Billy shouted desperately.

But none of them did. They were out of control and deaf to his pleas. Shouting and screaming. Fizzing and flashing. Doors clattered, racks rattled, wires writhed like a knot of snakes. The atmosphere was electric –

the floor was a mess.

"We won't stand it any more, will we Pongo?" yelled Freezer.

"We certainly won't," Fridge agreed, as the pair of them continued to eject the contents of their shelves. Smashed eggs, squashed tomatoes, spilt milk and frozen peas lay in a sloppy, slippery mess in front of their open doors. "And don't call me Pongo!"

"I'll never make another Chicken and Gooseberry Chasseur as long as I live!" roared the oven, as it singed anything that came too close with a blast of roasting air.

"Ouch, my poor nozzle!" groaned the vacuum cleaner, as it did just that.

"*Nerr-nerr-ni-nerr-nerr*," the food-mixer taunted, as the microwave zapped at it with a sudden bolt of

lightning. "Missed me, you missed me!"

The toaster glowed red-hot. "Don't worry, my love," it proclaimed. "I'll take you away from all this."

But the kettle was having none of it. "Don't you understand? It's the microwave I love. You're . . . you're . . . REVOLTING!" it screeched.

Billy trembled with fear. If he lived

to be 105 he would never, ever forget the scene before him that Saturday evening. The zap and dazzle. The gurgle and grunt. The scorching heat. The icy blast. The roaring, buzzing, screeching, squealing, crashing din of it all!

"Help . . . *mffflbluch!*" came a frantic voice from the far end of the kitchen.

Billy spun round – and gasped. A pair of legs in black tights were sticking out of the open dishwasher, kicking desperately.

"Mum!" Billy cried. He dashed forwards, grabbed her ankles and tugged as hard as he could.

At that moment, the cupboard door burst open and Mr Barnes came staggering backwards, the vacuum cleaner snapping at his heels. Its flex was coiled tightly around his neck.

"Billy," he wheezed, eyes bulging. "You've got to do someth . . ."

He slipped on a squashed tomato and came crashing down onto the pile of food.

Billy slumped on the floor, close to tears. It was a nightmare – a nightmare he could never wake up from.

"STOP IT!" he bellowed. "STOP IT AT ONCE!"

"Not likely!" the dishwasher bellowed back as it released another gush of icy water onto Mrs Barnes's head.

Billy turned to the table and chair in desperation. "I thought you were meant to be hyper-intelligent beings," he said. "There must be *something* you can do."

"To be honest, I'm not sure there is," said the table. "Not now it's gone so far."

"Derek's really done it this time," the chair added gloomily.

"For as it is written in the *Book of Krud*," said Kerek. "'Before mental tentacle use, *always* check that the off-switch works.'"

"You could at least *try*," said Billy crossly. "And if not for me or mum and dad, then for Silas . . ."

The table and chair pulsed with sudden alarm.

"The High Emperor of the Universe!" the table exclaimed.

"We must protect him!" muttered the chair nervously. "But where is he?"

"Splish-splosh," came a voice from behind them.

Billy spun round. The table and chair shuffled about for a better look. In the flashing light the three of them could just make out Silas. He was sitting next to the washing machine, gurgling with delight.

"Ooh, and how I do hate being loaded up with all those muddy jeans," the washing machine was saying to him. "But it's always a pleasure washing *your* clothes, my little soap-sud," it purred. "After all, you're the only one who ever talks to me. The only one who cares."

"Safe and sound," the table sighed with relief.

"Maybe," said Billy, ducking out of the way of one of Microwave's zapping lightning bolts. "But for how long?"

"Billy's right!" said the chair. "The High Emperor is in danger. He must be protected at all costs."

"Then we must morph back," said the table.

The chair shuddered. "Is there no other way?"

"Revenge!" whooshed the dishwasher.

"Respect!" roared the vacuum cleaner as it tightened its grip round Mr Barnes's neck and tried its best to suck him up into its dustbag.

"But I love you," sobbed the toaster.

"All right!" cried the chair. "We shall morph back. One . . . two . . . three . . ."

CLUNK!

All at once, and without any warning, the lights went out. The kitchen fell abruptly still. Then out of the darkness came a plaintive voice.

"Where are you?" It was Billy's mum.

"Over here," his dad replied. "Where are *you*?"

"I'm not sure . . . Have you got Silas?"

"No, I . . . Silas?"

"Splish-splosh?" came a questioning voice.

Billy listened intently, but this time the washing machine made no reply.

Chapter Five

"It's over," Billy murmured, and sighed with relief.

"Not yet it isn't," came a voice.

"Who said that?" Billy heard his dad asking in alarm.

"See what I mean?" said the voice.

Billy wheeled round. And there, pulsing red and purple in the darkness were two glowing, blobby heads. Kerek and Zerek had changed back after all. As he watched, they moved silently across the kitchen. One to the dishwasher. One to the fridge-freezer. Then two blobs glowed brighter than the rest. They fizzed, they pulsed – they elongated.

A moment later there was a second *clunk* and the lights came back on. The fridge-freezer began humming. The kettle came to the boil.

Billy turned to Kerek and Zerek, whose own mental tentacles were quivering brightly. "Wh . . . what happened?" he said.

Kerek shrugged. "I'm not sure . . ."

Just then the door flew open. "*Ta-da*!" came a triumphant voice. "I did it! I turned off the central electricity supply under the stairs. Genius, or what?"

Zerek sniffed. "You're still a giant fluffy blue kangaroo," he said.

"Oh," said Derek, somewhat dismayed.

"Never mind all that," said Billy. "What about my mum and dad?"

"They're fine," said Kerek.

"Fine?" said Billy. "Look at them! They're both all stiff!"

Kerek waved his mental tentacle at Billy. "We've made them inanimate," he said.

"Inanimate!" Billy exclaimed.

Kerek nodded. "The mental tentacle works in many ways," he said. "It can make a toaster come to life," he explained, and glared at Derek. "And it can turn a living person into a . . ."

"Toaster!" Billy exclaimed, staring at his stiff, motionless parents in horror.

"Not exactly," Kerek reassured him.

"For one thing, where would you

put the bread?" interrupted Derek.

"Shut up, Derek!" said Kerek. "Don't worry, Billy, it's only temporary."

"We'll put them both to bed," said Zerek. "When they wake up tomorrow morning they'll be as good as new . . ."

"And they won't remember a single thing," added Derek.

"Luckily for you," growled Zerek ominously.

By the time they got Mr and Mrs Barnes safely tucked up in bed, Billy was exhausted. It hadn't helped that Derek got Dad's head stuck in the banisters – and Mum kept making an odd pinging noise, like a pop-up toaster.

"It's nothing," Kerek reassured him.

Billy looked at his parents for a last time before leaving the room. Maybe the Blobheads were right. Maybe they would forget everything that had happened to them in the kitchen. Billy hoped they would – for everyone's sake.

One thing was certain, though. They would both be extremely puzzled to find themselves waking up fully dressed. Mr Barnes would wonder where the smashed eggs and squashed tomatoes had come from – and why he had so many splinters of wood in his hair. While Mrs Barnes would ask herself how she had come to have a slice of bread in each ear.

Thankfully, Billy also knew that they'd be too embarrassed to ask *him* – and since Silas was unable to give the game away, it looked as though the goings-on in the kitchen that particular Saturday evening would

remain a secret for ever.

When Billy arrived back at the kitchen, the place was spotless. Every trace of the mayhem had disappeared. He looked at the toaster, the kettle, the dishwasher . . . They all looked so . . . *lifeless*! And yet!

Billy turned back. "Night-night!" he said. "Sweet dreams!"

In his bedroom at last, Billy found that the Blobheads had put Silas to bed. He was already fast asleep.

"Thanks," said Billy. "And for cleaning up the kitchen."

"It was the least we could do," Kerek explained. "And we also cleaned and serviced all the electrical appliances. At least, Zerek and I did. Derek spent the whole time morphing back."

"Finally made it though, didn't I?" said Derek.

"More's the pity," said Zerek.

"I *said* I was sorry," said Derek. "And I'll never do it again. From now on my mental tentacle will remain closed down."

"Make sure it does," said Kerek.

"Or else!" said Zerek.

"Come on, you two," said Billy. "Derek said he was sorry. And no real harm's been done." He climbed into bed. "Night-night, Kerek, Zerek and Derek," he said.

"Good night, Billy," said Kerek.

"Good night, Billy," said Zerek.

"Actually, I feel a little peckish," said Derek. "I think I'll make myself a sandwich. Anyone else want anything?"

"Not for me," said Billy yawning.

"No, thanks," said Kerek and Zerek.

"Won't be long, then," said Derek as he left the room.

The Blobheads let their tentacle-arms go limp and closed their eyes. Billy switched the light off.

"That's all very well," came an indignant if squeaky voice. "But what about me? I'm STARVING!"

Billy sat bolt upright and switched the light back on again. The Blobheads' eyes snapped open.

"Who said that?" they all shouted at once.

"It was me," came the squeaky voice from the opposite side of the room.

All eyes fell on Kevin the hamster.

"He's been using his mental tentacle again," said Kerek.

"After all he said!" stormed Zerek.

"And hamsters aren't like toasters or kettles," said Billy. "They don't have off-switches!"

The three of them looked at each other for a moment.

"DEREK!"

SCHOOL STINKS!

P. S. For Joseph and Anna
C. R. For Jack

Chapter One

"Six wives!" said Billy, as he collected his history project together. "Why couldn't Henry VIII just have one wife?"

He looked through the pages of writing and drawings.

"It made the homework so difficult!" he complained.

"Difficult?" said Derek, chewing thoughtfully on a felt-tip pen. "But surely six wives would make the homework easier. One to cook. One to wash-up. One to vacuum the carpets . . ."

"I said *home*work not *house*work," said
Billy. "And that's the third pen you've
eaten."

"But the ink is really delicious," said
Derek. "Purple is my favourite."

Billy groaned. Blobheads! he thought.
They travel halfway across the galaxy in
search of the High Emperor of the
Universe – and end up eating all my felt-
tip pens.

"I'll tell mum and dad," he warned
Derek.

"No!" said Derek, his blobby head pulsing with alarm. "Your parents must never find out about us."

"Then leave my pens alone!" said Billy.

"Sssh!" Zerek hissed from the cot in the corner of the room. "It has taken 47.6 minutes to get the High Emperor off to sleep. I do not want him woken again."

"He's *not* the High Emperor," said Billy. "He's my baby brother, Silas, and . . ."

"Lights out, Billy!" Mr Barnes called from downstairs. "School tomorrow."

"OK, Dad," said Billy, as quietly as he could.

"Is Silas asleep?" asked Mrs Barnes.

"Yes," replied Billy. "But not for much longer if you keep shouting like that," he muttered.

"N'night then, Billy," they both called.

"Goodnight!" Kevin the hamster shouted back.

"And don't you start!" said Billy. "It's bad enough that the Blobheads turned you into a talking hamster, without you rabbiting away all night."

"Well, pardon me for being nocturnal," Kevin said huffily. "And I don't *rabbit*!"

"He *hamsters*. Don't you, Kevin?" said Derek.

"Will you all be quiet!" Zerek hissed.

"All *right*!" said Billy.

He climbed into bed. The Blobheads stood in a cluster in their sleeping-corner and rested their blobby heads together. Billy switched off the light and was just falling asleep, when . . .

"Billy?"

Billy sighed. "Be quiet, Kevin."

"It wasn't me," the hamster squeaked indignantly.

The light went on. Derek was standing at Billy's desk. "It wasn't me, either," he said guiltily.

"It was me," said Kerek from the sleeping-corner. "Why *do* you go to school?"

"To learn things," said Billy. "All children go to school."

"Pfff," said Zerek. "We Blobheads know everything there is to know five minutes after leaving the egg."

"And anything we're not sure of, the Great Computer tells us," added Kerek.

Billy snorted. "The same Great Computer that brought you all the way to my bedroom and then left you stranded here, right?"

"The Great Computer works in mysterious ways," said Kerek mysteriously. "It knew the High Emperor needed protecting from the wicked Followers of Sandra . . ."

"Yeah, yeah," Billy yawned. "Derek, get back in your corner. And go to sleep, all of you."

He switched off the light. The room fell still.

"Billy?" It was Kerek again.

The light went on again. Billy sat up. "*Now* what?"

"You did say *all* children go to school?"

Billy rubbed his eyes. "Yes."

"Every single one?"

"Yes!"

"Even the High Emperor?"

Billy groaned. "One day, yes," he said. "Even Silas."

On hearing this, the three Blobheads let out a cry of alarm and huddled together. Their blobby heads flashed and fizzed.

"What?" said Billy. "*What?*"

Kerek looked up. "It is decided," he announced. "If the High Emperor is to attend this educational establishment then we must check it out at the earliest possible occasion."

"You mean . . ." Billy began.

"We will come to school with you tomorrow morning."

"Oh no, you won't," said Billy firmly.

"Oh yes, we will," the Blobheads chorused.

"Oh no . . ."

"OI! You lot!" came an angry voice. It was Kevin. "Keep the noise down. You're worse than a gaggle of squabbling gerbils – and you complain about *me* being noisy!"

"OK!" said Billy. "Keep your fur on!"

With the light off once and for all, Billy rolled over and tried to go to sleep.

He started counting sheep. But the sheep turned into queens, hundreds of them, each one with a golden crown perched on top of a curiously blobby head . . .

Asleep at last, Billy didn't notice the blobs on Kerek and Zerek's heads, still flashing and fizzing. Nor did he hear the faint rustle of paper.

"Yum," Derek purred and smacked his lips. "Deee-licious!"

Chapter Two

At a quarter past eight the following morning, Mr Barnes called upstairs. "Hurry up, Billy! Your breakfast's getting cold."

"I'll be right down," said Billy, then added, "What is it?"

"Something nutritious to set you up for the day," came his dad's cheery voice. "Kipper Kedgeree on a bed of garlic pineapple."

Billy groaned. "I suppose cornflakes are out of the question," he muttered.

"And why are you lot looking so pleased with yourselves?" he said, turning on the three grinning Blobheads.

"Nothing," said Kerek.

"Nothing at all," said Zerek.

"I told you last night," said Billy. "You are *not* coming to school. Is that clear?"

The Blobheads nodded.

"Christmas clear," said Derek.

Billy laughed. "It's *crystal* clear," he corrected him.

Derek frowned. "What is?" he said.

"Billy!" Mr Barnes shouted. "I won't tell you again. I . . . Alison," he said. "What's the matter?"

"My monthly sales report," came Mrs Barnes's anxious reply. "I can't find it anywhere. And I'm late enough as it is . . . It was on the sideboard. Billy? Have you seen my sales report?"

"No, Mum," he called back.

Behind him, Billy heard Derek burp.

"Derek!" said Billy. "You haven't had Mum's report, have you?"

"Report? What report?" said Derek innocently.

"It's full of graphs and figures and all bound up in a big blue and orange folder," Billy explained.

"No, I haven't," said Derek. "Though it sounds scrummy."

Billy pointed at the corner of the Blobhead's mouth. "Then what's that?"

Derek removed a fragment of paper with his tentacle and examined it.

"Well?" said Billy.

"It's . . ." Derek faltered.

"It's all right!" Mrs Barnes exclaimed. "I've found it! Billy, if you want that lift to school, you'll have to come now!"

"Coming!" Billy ran to the door. "Whoops!" he said, skidding to a halt.

"Nearly forgot my history project." He dashed back to the desk and gasped.

It wasn't there!

He stared at Derek. "What *is* that on your tentacle?"

Derek gulped guiltily. "A bit of King Henry, I think."

"You haven't . . . You couldn't . . ." Billy spluttered. "Are you telling me you've *eaten* my homework?"

"Derek!" said Kerek sternly.

"Typical!" stormed Zerek.

Derek looked round at the three angry faces, and turned a deep shade of purple. "It wasn't my fault," he wailed. "All those delicious colours . . . I just couldn't help myself."

"What am I going to do?" said Billy. "It took me all weekend. I can't go to school without it. Mr Trubshaw'll go mad!"

"Never fear," said Zerek calmly. "It's at times like these that we Blobheads turn to the Great Computer." He unclipped the small black box from the back of his belt. "Right. We simply tap in the information required. What was it? Henry the twelfth and his nine wives?"

"Henry the *eighth*," said Billy. "And he had *six* wives."

"Never fear," Zerek said airily, and pressed a button. "The Great Computer will sort out the details."

As Billy watched, the black box hummed and whirred, and sheet after sheet of paper emerged – each one covered in facts, figures and pictures. Zerek collected them up and slipped them inside a folder. Billy was amazed. It looked like an exact replica of the history project that Derek had eaten.

"There," said Zerek. "What could be simpler?"

"Billy!" shouted Mrs Barnes. "I'm going *now*."

Billy snatched the folder, dashed downstairs, out of the front door and raced towards the car.

"Oh, for heaven's sake," said Mrs Barnes when he appeared. "Where's your hat, your scarf, your jacket? It's freezing!"

"I'll be all right," said Billy.

"Go and get them," said Mrs Barnes.

While his mum revved the engine impatiently, Billy raced back up the garden path, into the hall, grabbed his baseball cap, his Manchester United scarf and his padded jacket.

"Billy, your breakfast!" Mr Barnes called from the kitchen.

The cap burped quietly.

"Sorry, dad," said Billy. "No time."

"Another wonderful meal gone to waste," Mr Barnes complained. "I don't know why I bother. Slaving away over a hot stove . . ."

Beep! Beep!

"I'm *coming*!" Billy shouted.

As he climbed into the passenger seat, Mrs Barnes sped off.

"Sorry, love," she said. "But I can't afford to be late." She glanced round and frowned. "I don't remember seeing that hat before . . ."

Chapter Three

The bell had already rung when Mrs Barnes screeched to a halt in front of the school. Billy jumped out and trotted after the other late-comers.

"Nice hat, Billy," Gloria Wrigley giggled.

"Yeah, I didn't know it was fancy-dress today," Toyah Snipe tittered.

Billy did what he always did when Gloria and Toyah teased him. He ignored them.

It was only in the cloakroom when he

reached up to take his hat off that Billy discovered something was not quite right. It didn't *feel* like his baseball cap. He pulled it off. It didn't *look* like it either. Instead of the dark-blue cap with white stitching, he was holding a tall, purple top hat with red blobs.

"Waaaah!" he shouted.

"Waaaah!" yelled the hat, even louder.

"Kerek? Is that you?"

"Yes," came a voice. But not from the hat. It was the scarf talking.

"Zerek?"

"Present," said the jacket.

The hat chuckled. "It's me. Derek."

"You're all here," said Billy crossly. "And after everything I said!"

"We had to," said the scarf.

"Our mission is to ensure the well-being of the High Emperor," said the jacket.

"And I thought it might be a giggle," the hat added.

Billy shrugged. "It could be worse," he said. "At least you haven't turned into a giant fluffy blue kangaroo like you usually do, Derek."

"'Ere, Billy Barnes," came a voice. "What's going on?"

Billy turned to see Warren Endecott

standing in the doorway. He groaned. Of all the boys and girls at Juniper Street Juniors, Warren was the last person Billy wanted to meet. He was big. He was mean. No one messed with Warren Endecott.

"Pardon?" said Billy innocently.

"You were talking to your hat," said Warren.

Billy smiled nervously. "'Course I wasn't."

"You called it Derek," said Warren, moving closer. "Anyway, why are you wearing such a weird hat in the first place?"

"I . . . errm . . ." Billy was floundering. He looked at the blobby top hat. "It's my dad's. I was in a hurry. I put it on by mistake."

"By mistake?" said Warren. "*That*!"

Just then, Derek panicked. Suddenly,

instead of the blobby top hat, Billy found himself clutching a fluffy blue beret.

Warren's eyes nearly popped out of his head. "How did you do that?" he said.

"Do what?" Billy bluffed.

But Warren knew what he'd seen. He seized the beret. "Let's have a closer look," he said.

"NO!" Billy cried, and tried to snatch it back.

"Gerroff! said Warren gruffly and shoved him away. He inspected the beret, tugging, squeezing, prodding . . . "There must be a secret button or something. If I can just . . ."

"Waaaah!" squealed the beret. "That hurt!"

Warren jumped back. "What was *that*?" He turned on Billy. "Something odd's going on here," he said, his fists

clenching menacingly. "And you'd better tell me what it is. Or else!"

"I . . . errm . . . Ventriloquism," Billy said. "I've been learning how to throw my voice."

Warren pushed his face into Billy's. "Are you taking the mickey?" he said. "'Coz if you are, I'm going to pulp you, Billy Barnes. I'm going to pulverize you . . ."

"You don't understand," said Billy, weakly.

"Calling me thick, now, eh? Right, that's it . . ."

"Don't worry, Billy," came a small, yet determined voice. "Leave this to us."

As he heard the words, Billy also noticed a movement. The scarf round his neck was uncoiling and reaching down into the left-hand pocket of his jacket.

"The other side," the jacket hissed.

Warren's jaw dropped.

The end of the scarf reappeared. It was wrapped around what looked like a perfume bottle filled with purple liquid.

"What the . . .?" gasped Warren and Billy together.

"Hold your nose, Billy," shouted the scarf.

Billy did as he was told.

Warren had had enough. "You bloom-ing weirdo!" he roared, and lunged forwards. "I'm gonna . . ."

"Now!" cried the jacket.

The scarf reared up, pushed the little bottle into Warren's face and removed the stopper. Warren's nose twitched. The stopper was popped back into place.

"D'ya know what, Billy Barnes?" said

Warren, his big fist resting on Billy's shoulder.

"Wh . . . what?" stammered Billy.

"You're the nicest boy in the whole school," he gushed, and a great gormless grin spread across his face. "Will you be my friend?"

"Your friend?" said Billy.

"Oh, please say you will."

"Just give me back my hat, Warren," said Billy.

Warren looked down at the beret. He held it out then, just as Billy was about to take it, snatched it back coyly. "Only if you promise me something."

"What?" asked Billy.

"Promise you'll play skipping with me at break-time."

"Skipping?"

"I *love* skipping," said Warren. "Oh, go on. Please."

"OK, then," Billy nodded. "I promise."

"Oh, thank you, Billy!" Warren cried. "Till break-time, then." And with that, he turned on his toes and tripped off to class.

The moment Warren was gone, Billy pulled off the scarf and the jacket and hung them on his hook with his hat. "You shouldn't have come here," he said angrily.

"Don't worry about us," said the jacket.

"I'm not!" said Billy. "I'm worried about everyone else in the school. What *have* you done to Warren?"

"Clever, eh?" said the beret, as it morphed into a pirate's tricorn hat. "It's called *Psychopong*."

"*Psychopong?*" Billy shouted.

"Or *psycho-morpho-blobby-pong*," to give it its full name," the jacket explained. "It's a mood modifier. We never go any-where without it."

"It is useful when some of the more irrational species on Blob get out of hand," said the scarf. "But enough of this. You go to your lesson. We'll take a look round."

"Not with that stuff, you don't!" said Billy, snatching the bottle away from the scarf. He slipped it into his trouser

153

pocket. "You've done more than enough already."

"Spoilsport," said the tricorn hat sulkily.

"Wait here till I get back," said Billy. "And I don't want to hear a peep out of you."

"A peep?" said the jacket. "Why would the most hyper-intelligent creatures in the universe wish to go *peep*? We can talk, you know."

"Well, don't!" Billy snapped. "Just stay silent. I'll come back at break-time."

The tricorn giggled. "You're playing skipping with Warren at break-time," it reminded him.

Billy groaned.

"It's OK," said the scarf. "The effects of *Psychopong* are strictly temporary. By break-time he'll probably want to beat you up instead."

154

Fighting or skipping with Warren Endecott? What a choice!

Billy wasn't sure which was worse.

Chapter Four

"Right," said Mr Trubshaw. "Your history projects. Did you all get them finished?"

"Yes, sir," came the hissing chorus.

"And I enjoyed every minute of it," Warren Endecott added, smiling sweetly.

"Quite," said Mr Trubshaw uncertainly. He looked round. "Who'd like to read out their work?"

"Me, sir! Me!" Warren cried eagerly.

Mr Trubshaw ignored him.

"Billy," he said. "How about you?"

Billy pulled the papers from his folder

and stepped up to the front of the classroom. He cleared his throat.

"Herbert the Eighth and his fourteen and a half wives lived in an extremely large house in . . ."

Billy stopped, aghast. *This* wasn't the homework he'd slaved over all weekend. His knees shook. His palms sweated. And, as a ripple of sniggering went round the room, his face turned bright red.

Voice quavering, he continued. "The number of wives proved very helpful when it came to housework. There was a wife for every chore. One for . . . the ironing." Billy swallowed. "One for . . ."

"Billy Barnes!" Mr Trubshaw bellowed. "What is the meaning of this? I've never heard such twaddle! This is . . . This is . . ."

Billy couldn't meet his teacher's stern gaze. He felt sick. He felt scared. The sniggering grew louder.

He knew he shouldn't. He knew it was foolish. But there was nothing else for it . . . Billy reached into his pocket. His fingers closed around the bottle.

"This is . . ." Mr Trubshaw roared for a third time.

Holding his breath, Billy whipped the *Psychopong* out, pushed it up to Mr Trubshaw's nose and removed the stopper for a second.

" . . . brilliant!" Mr Trubshaw exclaimed. "Inventive, imaginative – an absolute masterpiece."

The boys and girls of class 4T looked at one another in amazement.

"Never have I heard such a beautiful introduction to a history project." He wiped his eyes and sniffed. "I feel quite

overcome. I must . . . leave the room," he sobbed.

"Can we go and play skipping?" called Warren.

But Mr Trubshaw was gone. The sound of him trumpeting into his handkerchief echoed from the corridor. As Billy returned to his seat, everyone spoke at once.

"What did you do? What was that stuff?"

Gloria Wrigley tapped him on the shoulder. "Come on, Billy," she giggled. "You can tell me."

"No," said Billy.

"Oh, Billy," she wheedled. "Just . . ."

"Got it!" came a cry. While Gloria had kept him busy, Toyah had picked his pocket. She held up the bottle triumphantly.

"What is it?" said Gloria.

"Give it back!" shouted Billy.

"Perfume, I think," Toyah tittered. "Billy, you *shouldn't* have . . ."

She put it to her nose. Billy leapt forwards. "Don't!" he cried.

But it was too late.

Toyah removed the stopper and breathed in. The effect was instant. She turned on Billy and grabbed him by the lapels.

"Hey, dog-breath!" she bellowed.

"Fancy a knuckle-sandwich?" She drew her fist back threateningly.

"Oh, don't hit him!" Warren pleaded. "He's my best friend. We're playing skipping later."

"Put the stopper back in the bottle," said Billy, trying to remain calm. "Before things get out of control . . ."

But at that moment, Gloria made a grab for the bottle. Toyah spun round and threw a punch. As she did so, the bottle slipped from her grasp and crashed to the floor. The purple liquid spilled out and began to evaporate before their eyes.

At that moment, the door flew open and in flapped a jacket, a hat and a scarf. While the children stared, open-mouthed, the scarf jumped up, wound itself around Billy's neck and dragged him from the room, with the jacket and

hat close behind. The jacket slammed the door shut. The hat, now a gigantic red Santa bobble hat, bounced up and down.

"Red alert!" it squealed, and started to make a noise like a police siren.

"What the . . .?" said Billy.

"The situation is critical," the jacket shouted above the din.

"The door must be kept shut!" added

the scarf. "The effects will wear off eventually. I hope."

"You *hope*!" said Billy. "But . . ."

Kerek pointed at the window in the door. The classroom was full of purple mist.

"They've had too much," said Zerek.

"Far more than we'd give even the wildest boggle-beastie on Blob," said Kerek.

At the other end of the corridor, the headteacher's door burst open, and a short, portly woman in a tweed suit bustled out. It was Mrs Bleasdale. She looked confused.

"What is all that noise?" she yelled.

"Shut up, Derek!" Billy hissed.

The siren abruptly stopped. Mrs Bleasdale approached briskly.

"Ah, Billy," she said. "Whatever have you done to Mr Trubshaw? He's in my office in floods of tears over a magnificent piece of work you've done. I really must read it myself." She frowned. "But why aren't you in class? And where did you get that ridiculous hat?"

"I . . . errm . . ."

"Never mind that now," said Mrs Bleasdale. "Back inside with you. I'll be taking the rest of Mr Trubshaw's lesson."

Before Billy could warn her, the head-teacher seized the door handle and

marched into the classroom. The swirling purple mist poured out.

"Run, Billy!" came three insistent voices in unison.

Billy spun round. As he did so, the scarf, the jacket and the hat morphed back into Kerek, Zerek – and a giant fluffy blue kangaroo.

"Oh, Derek!" Billy exclaimed. "Not again!"

"Hold your nose!" said Kerek urgently. "And RUN!"

Billy, Kerek and Zerek dashed down to the bottom of the corridor, with the giant fluffy blue kangaroo bringing up the rear.

"This way," Billy yelled. He skidded round to the right and continued to the fire exit. The Blobheads went with him. Billy pushed the bar on the door, they all ran out and, *slam*!

"Phew!" said Kerek.

"Thank Blob," said Zerek.

"Where's Derek?" said Billy, looking round.

Zerek tutted. "Trust him!"

The three of them pressed their faces against the window and peered into the corridor. There was the giant fluffy blue kangaroo, wandering about with its paws clamped over its nose.

"Over here!" yelled Billy and hammered on the window.

At that moment, Mrs Pettifogg the school secretary appeared round the corner, eyes streaming and a handkerchief pressed to her nose, and ran straight into Derek.

"What the . . .?" she exclaimed. She seized Derek's fluffy blue ear in her vice-like grip. "You bust have got id

through the kitcheds. Those bloob-
bigg didder ladies," she complained.
"I'll have to call the authorities."

And with that, she dragged him
back along the corridor.

"She can't!" Billy exclaimed.

"She already has," said Zerek
glumly.

"But the *Psychopong*," said Billy.
"Why hasn't it affected her?"

From inside came the sound of a muffled sneeze.

"With that awful cold?" said Kerek. "She can't smell a thing."

Chapter Five

The *Psychopong* had by now spread to every corner of the school. As Billy, Kerek and Zerek crept round the outside of the building, the scene through every window was one of utter chaos.

5P was bad. 6L was worse. Dancing. Shouting. Fighting.

"I'm a little flower!" came the gruff voice of the biggest boy.

"Do that again, Hermione, I'll break your legs," screamed a pale girl with blonde curls.

"Stop calling me names," said Mr Lander, "or I'll tell."

With a groan, Billy moved to the next window. Behind it was his own class. He gasped. If 5P was bad and 6L was worse, then 4T was as awful as it could possibly be.

Mrs Bleasdale was up on the front table – tweed skirt tucked into her pink knickers – conducting an aerobics class. "Jump and twist and *turn!*" she squealed enthusiastically.

Not that anyone was paying any attention. Gloria and Toyah were scrapping in the middle of the floor. Lucy Williams had Bruce Tully in a savage headlock.

"I want my mummy," he was howling.

The Taggart twins – the brainiest boys in the class – were being a train, chuffing happily up and down the aisles. Prim

170

Amelia Tilly was entertaining anyone who would listen with her musical burps. And Warren was racing frantically round the class with a skipping rope pleading for someone – *anyone* – to skip with him.

"You must stop this," Billy told the Blobheads.

"It won't be easy," said Kerek. "*Psycho-pong* is powerful stuff. As the *Book of Krud* warns us, 'Beware, for while a little *Psychopong* will modify the mangiest mood, too much will mangle the mind completely!'"

"But you've got to do something before the authorities arrive," said Billy desperately. "What about your Great Computer? I thought it could do anything."

From inside the classroom came a loud crash as Mrs Bleasdale lost her footing and plummeted to the floor. Luckily for the headteacher, her fall was broken. Unluckily for Warren, *he* broke it. The pair of them ended up sprawling on the floor, tangled up in the skipping rope.

"Will *you* play skipping with me?" Warren asked hopefully.

Billy turned on Kerek. "NOW!" he yelled.

Kerek removed the small black box from his belt and began stabbing at the buttons. The screen lit up and bleeped. He pressed some more buttons. Then some more . . .

"Well?" said Billy.

"There is something," said Kerek. "An antidote . . ."

Zerek squinted at the screen. "Of course," he said.

"What?" said Billy.

"*Psychopong* is a complex chemical compound," said Kerek. "To neutralize its effects we need an unbound emulsifying polymer."

"And have you got any?" said Billy.

The Blobhead shook his head.

"But what *is* it?" said Billy.

"It's sweet and yellow," said Kerek. "And milky thick."

"Derek had some for breakfast the other night," Zerek added.

For a moment, Billy looked confused. Then it dawned on him. "CUSTARD!" he shouted.

Holding their noses, Billy, Kerek and Zerek charged through the delivery door of the school kitchen. The dinner ladies didn't notice. They were all too engrossed in the rowdy football songs they were chanting.

"There's an Arsenal supporter in the storeroom!" Billy yelled.

With a cry of "let's get him!" the five women bundled inside. Zerek slammed the door and bolted it securely.

"Right," Billy announced. "You get started on the custard."

"And you?" said Zerek.

"I'm going to open every window in the school," he shouted as he rushed off. "And find out where Derek is."

While the school echoed and shook with the continuing madness, Kerek mixed 3.6 kilograms of custard powder with 1.8 kilograms of sugar and stirred it all into a thick paste with some milk. Meanwhile, Zerek filled an enormous pot with the rest of the 56 litres of milk, and brought it to the boil. Then, as Kerek poured one into the other, Zerek stirred vigorously with a wooden spoon. The thickening custard splattered every-where.

"Mrs Pettifogg has got Derek locked in the stationery cupboard," said Billy, running back into the kitchen. "She's standing guard outside with a broom muttering something about giant rats, and that the authorities are on their way! We've got no time to lose . . ." He looked at the bubbling custard. "Are you sure this is going to work?"

Kerek dipped a tentacle into the custard and tasted it. "There's only one way to find out."

By the time they lugged the huge pot of custard to the serving-hatch, the Great Computer revealed that the *Psychopong* had finally cleared – even if its effects were continuing.

Billy stopped holding his nose and chalked up the day's menu on the black-board. *Custard. Custard. Custard.* Then he grabbed the handbell and rang it at the dining-hall entrance.

From every part of the school, a cry went up and the corridors were suddenly jam-packed with famished pupils and teachers.

"Grub's up!" cried Mrs Bleasdale.

"Lunchy-poos!" shouted the Taggart twins.

"Oh, but I must think of my figure," said Warren.

"Out of my way!" roared Toyah.

"Stop pushing, or I'll tell," Mr Lander complained.

They burst into the dining-hall.

"CUSTARD!" everyone cried out on seeing the board, not stopping to look at the two blobby figures at the counter.

Dressed up in their dinner-lady outfits of green coats and white lacy caps, the two Blobheads could hardly keep up with the demand.

Billy slipped nervously in beside the Taggart twins and watched to see if the antidote would really work. There couldn't be much time left before the authorities arrived.

Gradually, one by one, eyelids began to droop, heads nodded, shoulders slumped. Warren's face plopped down

into his bowl of custard. The hall was silent but for the low rumble of gurgly snores.

"When they wake up again, everyone will be back to normal," said Kerek.

"I'll believe that when I see it," said Billy.

DDDRRRIIINNNGGG!

At the sound of the school bell, everyone's eyes snapped open.

"Billy Barnes!" came a voice. Billy looked round. It was Mr Trubshaw. "I haven't forgotten that atrocious piece of homework," he said. "I'll see you later."

"Yeah, me too," growled Warren Endecott, wiping custard from his ear.

"Kerek was right," Billy sighed. "Every-one *is* back to normal."

"'Ere we go! 'Ere we go! 'Ere we go!" came a chorus of raucous voices from the back of the kitchen.

"Who on earth is that?" asked Mrs Bleasdale.

"Neber bind that," said Mrs Pettifogg, striding into the dining-hall. "The authorities are here. I thig you'll want to see this, Headbistress."

"Me, too," said Billy, picking up the blobby coat and scarf on the counter, and following them out of the hall.

A moment later, Mrs Pettifogg, Mrs Bleasdale, Billy and Mr Smeal – a thin, balding man from the council with a net – were all standing in front of the locked door of the stationery cupboard.

"A bonstrous great rat," Mrs Pettifogg was saying. "Two betres tall, at least! But I banaged to pid it dowd."

"All right, madam," said Mr Smeal importantly. "Stand back. I'll deal with this."

He stepped forwards, net raised. He

turned the key in the lock. He turned the handle, pushed the door open and . . .

"Good grief! How on earth did that get in there?" said Billy, picking up a small blobby bobble hat from the floor.

Mr Smeal looked disappointed. Mrs Bleasdale turned to Mrs Pettifogg. "I must say, Muriel, your behaviour today has been most peculiar!"

*

Later that evening, Billy was finishing his re-written history project – Mr Trubshaw had insisted – when the Blobheads came bustling into the bedroom.

"School indeed!" Kerek was saying.

"The poor High Emperor," said Zerek. "I don't envy him."

"Oh, I don't know," said Derek. "I thought it was a giggle."

"So, what did you learn about?" asked Kevin the hamster.

Kerek and Zerek smiled. "Custard," they said.

"Custard?" said Derek. "Did I miss custard? Oh, I love custard. Though . . ."

Billy was collecting his papers together. Derek sidled over towards him and looked over his shoulders. "Mmm," he said and smacked his lips. "That looks nice."

"Derek!" roared Kerek and Zerek.

"You leave my homework alone!" shouted Billy.

"What?" said Derek, looking hurt. "Anyone would think I was going to *eat* it!"

BEWARE
OF THE
BABYSITTER

P. S. For Anna and Joseph
C. R. For William

Chapter One

"Have you seen my head anywhere, darling?" Mr Barnes called up from the hall.

"It's where you left it," came the reply. "On the settee."

Mr Barnes hurried into the sitting room, put the head on and bounded upstairs. He went into the bedroom Billy shared with his baby brother, Silas. The two boys were sitting on the carpet beside a bucket, a trombone and an ironing board.

"How do I look?" said Mr Barnes.

"Like a giant gerbil," Kevin the hamster piped up from his cage.

"A gerbil?" he said.

"Gorilla, I mean," Billy broke in hurriedly. "Did I say gerbil?" He laughed awkwardly. "You look brilliant, Dad."

"Thanks," said Mr Barnes uncertainly. "I must say, you're getting very good at that voice-throwing lark. I could have sworn Kevin spoke just then."

Billy gave the hamster a filthy look. "I've been practising a lot," he said.

"Uh-huh," said Mr Barnes. He nodded towards the bucket, trombone and ironing board. "And what are these things doing here?"

"They're . . . um . . . for my hobby," said Billy.

"What, ventriloquism?" said Mr Barnes.

"Y . . . yes."

Mr Barnes shook his head. "You're a strange boy, Billy Barnes," he said.

"What do you expect with a gorilla for a father?" retorted Kevin the hamster.

Mr Barnes chuckled. "Yes, very good, Billy," he said. "Keep practising."

"I need zipping up," Mrs Barnes called from along the landing.

"I'll be right there," said Mr Barnes. He turned back to Billy. "Could you get Silas into his cot for me?" he asked. "And make sure this lot's cleared away before you go to bed."

"You're the boss," said Kevin.

The moment Mr Barnes was out of earshot, Billy spun round and glared at the hamster. "Can't you ever keep quiet?" he said.

"Well, excuse me!" said Kevin huffily. "I thought he was talking to both of us."

Billy groaned. "A talking hamster! As if my life wasn't complicated enough hiding three aliens in my bedroom, they had to go and make you talk. Thanks a lot, fellas!" said Billy.

The bucket, trombone and ironing board morphed back into the three Blobheads – Kerek, Zerek and Derek. The purple and red blobs on their heads pulsed brightly.

"And why can't you disguise yourself more sensibly?" said Billy. "As a football, or skittles, or a jigsaw – something you'd expect to find in a kid's bedroom. I mean, honestly! You've travelled halfway across the galaxy in search of the High Emperor of the Universe who, for some crazy reason, you think is my baby brother, Silas. You've got gadgets and gizmos coming out of your ears—"

"We haven't got ears," interrupted Zerek sulkily. "We have listening-blobs." He turned away.

"You know what I mean," said Billy.

"Blimey, you reckon you're hyper-intelligent beings, but—"

"He caught us by surprise," said Kerek stiffly.

"But an ironing board!" exclaimed Billy.

"Yes, what luck!" said Derek. "I had no idea ironing boards were so useful for practising that ventril . . . ventrillionoquism . . . ism . . ."

"They're not!" Billy said, exasperated. "I only said *that* because . . . Oh, never mind. You heard Dad, let's get Silas to bed."

"I already have," said Zerek. Billy turned and saw Silas snuggled up sleepily in his cot. "Who's a lovely ikkle High Emperor?" Zerek murmured as he tickled the gurgling infant under the chin with one of his tentacles. "I do have my uses," he sniffed.

"I know," said Billy more softly. "Just try to blend in a bit better next time you morph."

"What, like your father?" said Kerek. "Morphing into a big monkey when he's supposed to be taking your mother out tonight. I don't call that blending in."

"Dad? Morph?" said Billy and burst out laughing.

"But we all saw him," said Kerek, puzzled.

"Plain as the nose on your plate," said Derek.

Billy laughed even louder. "Plain as the nose on your face!" he corrected him.

"There's nothing plain about *my* nose," said Derek, hotly.

At that moment, the front doorbell rang. Mr Barnes ran along the landing, past the open bedroom door.

"Are you telling me that is *not* a big monkey?" said Kerek.

"You don't understand," said Billy. "It's just a costume!"

"A costume?"

"He's dressed up in a gorilla suit," Billy explained. "They're going to a fancy-dress party at Mum's work. The Jungle Ball. That's probably the babysitter arriving now."

Mrs Tarzan flashed past the doorway and followed her husband down the stairs.

Zerek whisked Silas up in his tentacles. "Baby*sitter*?" he said nervously. "I don't like the sound of that."

"It sounds dangerous," Kerek agreed.

"Dangerous?" said Billy.

"Sitting on babies," said Kerek. "*I* wouldn't like to be sat on."

Derek sniggered. "Don't you know anything, Kerek?" he said smugly. "A babysitter is one of those plastic things Billy's father is always trying to get the High Emperor to sit on."

"Actually, that's a potty," said Billy. "A babysitter is someone who comes to look after you when your parents go out." He frowned. "I haven't met this one before. But I hope she's nicer than Mrs Jarvis. She smelled of stale biscuits and old bananas . . ."

Derek licked his lips. "Sounds delicious," he said.

"*And* she made me go to bed at half-past seven!" Billy complained.

Kerek was frowning. "Haven't met this one before?" he repeated. "Are you saying your parents are leaving you with a stranger?"

Billy shrugged. "She's Mum's secretary's daughter," he said. "She's seventeen. She's meant to be very nice . . ."

But the Blobheads were no longer listening. Kerek and Zerek stood together, their blobby heads fizzing and pulsating, while Derek scurried round the room shouting.

"Stranger alert! Stranger alert!" he wailed.

"Calm down!" Billy hissed. "There's nothing to worry about."

"So you say," said Kerek. "But we have travelled far to protect the High Emperor of the Universe, for he is in great danger from the wicked Followers of Sandra! They would stop at nothing to—"

"How many times do I have to tell you?" Billy interrupted. "Silas is not the High Emperor of the Universe. He's my little brother! And as for this Sandra you keep going on about. How can you protect anyone from her and her followers if you don't even know what she looks like?"

"*It*, not *she*," said Kerek shuddering. "And, as we've told you before, Sandra can take on many shapes. That is why we must be vigilant at all times." He paused. "Yet we have seen Sandra's true form," he added. "It is grotesque. Huge and pink—"

"With twenty-six arms," said Zerek. "Eight glowing eyes, breath that can stun a wild boggle-beastie at a hundred paces—"

"And appalling taste in music," Derek added.

"So quite difficult to spot!" said Kevin the hamster.

"Sandra is merciless, cruel and hard," Zerek continued. "It enslaves whole worlds, forcing them to dance to its terrible tunes. Why, if it ever got its hands on the High Emperor it could take over the universe."

The three Blobheads shivered with horror.

"Billy," Mrs Barnes called up. "The babysitter's here. Come down and meet Sandra."

"Waaaah!" the Blobheads screeched in unison. "WAAAAAH!"

Chapter Two

"Billy!" Mr Barnes shouted. "Stop practising and get down here. We don't want to be late."

"Coming," Billy yelled back. He turned on the Blobheads furiously. "Be quiet!" he hissed. "Or do you want them to find out you're living in my bedroom?"

For a moment, the Blobheads went silent. But only for a moment. "You do not understand the gravity of the situation," said Kerek, rushing towards the bathroom. "Sandra is here. We must do everything we can to protect the High Emperor. It mustn't discover his hiding place."

"Great hiding place," said Kevin the hamster. "In a cot in his own bedroom. The last place a babysitter would think to look."

"Hmm," said Derek. "I thought underneath the socks in Billy's cupboard might be better, but if you think the cot is safer . . ."

"*Nowhere* is safe from Sandra," said Zerek ominously.

"But Sandra is just her name," said Billy. "There are thousands of Sandras—"

"And that's supposed to make me feel better?" said Zerek. "Just the word is enough to make my tentacles curl."

"*Billy!*" his dad shouted. "I won't tell you again."

"I've got to go," said Billy. "Don't do anything silly. I'll be back soon."

"But you can't go down there!" said Zerek. "*It's* down there."

"If *I* don't go down, then *it* will come up," said Billy.

"Waaaah!" said Zerek. "What are you waiting for? Go on!"

"Stop!" said Kerek, as he dashed back from the bathroom. "You must protect yourself. Take these," he said, stuffing a tentacleful of cotton wool balls down Billy's jumper. "And this." He gave him a bottle of his dad's *Cool Sweat* aftershave. "Put it in your back pocket."

Billy shrugged. "If it makes you feel better," he said.

"BILLY!"

*

"At last!" said Mr Barnes when Billy finally appeared.

"Sorry," he said. "But you asked me to put Silas to bed. I was just settling him."

Mr Barnes, who was holding his gorilla head under his arm, smiled sheepishly. "Ah yes . . . erm . . . good boy."

"Is he asleep already," asked Mrs Barnes, "with all that racket you were making?"

"Sound asleep," Billy said innocently. "All tucked up in his cot."

Mrs Barnes turned to Sandra. "This is Billy," she told her. "Billy, Sandra Smethwick." She glanced at her watch. "We really must be going. Be good, Billy. We won't be late back."

She turned to go.

"And do help yourself to some of my kipper and honey quiche," said Mr Barnes as he followed her out.

The door closed. Sandra turned to Billy and patted him on the shoulder.

"I'm sure we're going to get on just fine," she said. Billy winced. Her breath smelt of gas. "I . . . *whoooargh!*" Sandra suddenly recoiled as her fingers grazed a stray cotton wool ball

204

at his neck. Half a dozen more fell out of the bottom of his jumper and landed at his feet. "What are those?" she hissed.

Billy turned red. "Cotton wool balls," he said. "I was just . . . erm . . . practising ventriloquism: cotton wool, very useful . . ."

"Just clear them away," said Sandra sharply. "At once."

Billy crouched down to collect the little white fluffy balls. As he did so, the bottle in his back pocket fell to the floor and the smell of aftershave wafted up.

"And what is that disgusting pong?" she said.

Billy looked at the bottle with mock surprise. "I wonder how that got there?"

Sandra's nose wrinkled. "Well, I'm sure your dad wouldn't want you wasting his expensive aftershave. Go and put it back where you found it. And, if you don't mind, I'll put some music on – I brought my own tapes."

Billy nodded uncertainly. "I'll be back in a minute," he said as he dashed upstairs.

"Well?" said Kerek, the moment Billy walked into the bedroom. "What happened?"

"I spilt the aftershave," said Billy crossly. "That's what happened."

"And how did it react?" asked Zerek.

"It? You mean Sandra?" said Billy. "She called Dad's *Cool Sweat* a disgusting pong."

"But it didn't keel over and start frothing at the mouth?" said Kerek.

"'Fraid not," said Billy.

Kerek shook his head miserably. "We're going to need something stronger. And the cotton wool balls?"

"She didn't like them either," said Billy. "She must think I'm a complete idiot."

"That makes two of us," said Kevin.

"She didn't like the aftershave or the cotton wool!" Zerek exclaimed. "Don't you see?"

"No," said Billy. "I don't."

"You would if you read the *Book of Krud*," said Kerek importantly. "For it is written there, in Section 3, Paragraph vii – 'Sticks and stones won't break its bones, so whiffs and fluff's the answer.' *Now* do you see?"

"Not really," said Billy.

"Sandra is terrified of all things soft and fluffy," Kerek explained. "And nice smells make her sick!"

Billy raised his eyes to the ceiling. "She's just a babysitter whose name happens to be Sandra," he said.

The Blobheads weren't convinced.

"Was there anything else suspicious?" Zerek persisted.

Billy laughed. "No," he said. "Unless you call stinky breath suspicious—"

"Stinky breath!" all three Blobheads cried out at once.

"I told you!" said Zerek. "It *must* be

Sandra! She shall not sit on Silas! She's got to go!"

"Stop it at once!" said Billy angrily. "You're being ridiculous."

At that moment, Sandra's music floated up from the sitting room.

"*Ooby-dooby do!*
I love you!
Way-hey-hey!
You're OK!"

Billy winced. It was the worst song he had ever heard. The Blobheads quivered like jelly and clamped their tentacles over their listening-blobs.

"The music!" gasped Derek.

"I know, I know," said Billy. "But just because she's got bad breath and rotten taste in music, it does not make her a monster from outer space. She's got two arms and two eyes, just like everybody else."

"Of course," said Kerek. "Like your dad!"

Billy frowned. Now what was he going on about?

"It's just a costume," said Kerek.

"A costume?" said Billy.

"It's dressed up in a babysitter suit."

Billy had heard enough. "That's it!" he hissed. "Get into your sleeping corner, all of you. I don't want to hear another peep out of you."

As he left the room and stomped down the stairs, the music grew louder. Billy groaned.

"Come back, Mrs Jarvis," he muttered. "All is forgiven."

Chapter Three

Three hours later, everything seemed OK. There was no noise from upstairs. Unfortunately, it was the noise downstairs that was the problem. First the collected hits of a boy-band – Smooch – followed by Sister Ingrid and her singing sheep. Now it sounded as if someone was trying to push a piano down a flight of stairs while someone else hammered nails into a wall. Sandra lay on the sofa with her eyes shut and a dreamy smile on her face.

Billy crossed the room and turned the music down low. "Sandra," he said.

"What is it?" said Sandra evenly.

"There's something I want to ask you."

Sandra's eyes remained closed. "Yes?" she said.

"Would you mind if I watched television? *Casualty Ward Thirteen* is on. It's my favourite."

This wasn't exactly true, but anything was better than the dying piano and mad hammer.

Sandra nodded. "If you must," she said.

Billy picked up the remote control and zapped the TV into action. Three paramedics in green overalls were dashing down a long hospital corridor with a stretcher. Suddenly, the scene changed and a blobby-headed news-reader appeared on the screen.

"We interrupt this episode of *Casualty Ward Thirteen* with an important message. Would Sandra Smethwick return home without delay. Go home, Sandra. Now . . ."

Billy tutted with exasperation. The Blobheads were up to their tricks again. As he zapped the control to

change channels he glanced round at Sandra – luckily she didn't seem to have noticed a thing.

Back on the television screen, a carpet warehouse advert was coming to an end. Billy sat back in the settee.

A second blobby-headed character appeared. "Is your name Sandra? Then you have won two tickets to a secret destination on the other side of the world," he announced. "Flights leave in twenty minutes. So hurry . . ."

"Oh, this is hopeless," Billy muttered as he switched the television off.

Sandra opened one eye. "Anything the matter?" she said.

"N . . . no," said Billy. He smiled awkwardly. "But there's nothing much on. Maybe I'll read a book."

Just then the phone rang. "Shall I get that?" asked Sandra.

"OK," said Billy. The next instant an awful thought occurred to him. He leapt from the settee. "No!" he shouted, and elbowed her out of the way. "*I'll* get it."

He picked up the receiver and held it tentatively to his ear.

"Radio Whoosh FM invite you to meet fabulous boy-band Smooch at our studios in Ballycahoona," came a voice. "This awesome experience can be yours if you can answer one simple question . . . Is your name Sandra?"

"NO!" Billy yelled and slammed the phone down. He turned to Sandra. "Wrong number," he said.

"Hmmph!" Sandra snorted, her revolting breath hitting him full blast in the face. "You could say sorry for shoving me like that."

Before Billy could say a single word

– apology or otherwise – the door burst open. He and Sandra spun round. Two fluffy toys marched across the carpet towards them, followed by a blobby plastic potty on wheels.

"Go home! Go home!" chanted the koala.

"Get out!" demanded the kitten.

"And don't come back!" shouted the plastic potty.

Sandra turned to Billy with a look of absolute horror on her face.

"They're my baby brother's," Billy explained. "Battery-powered," he added hastily, looking down at the potty. "What will they think of next?"

"I don't care whose they are," Sandra said sternly. "Take them away."

Billy didn't need telling twice. He strode forwards, picking up the koala and the kitten with one hand and

grabbing the plastic potty with the other. Then he said to Sandra what he always said to his parents when the Blobheads' antics made them think they were going mad.

"You wait here, and I'll get you a nice cup of tea."

"What *are* you playing at?" Billy stormed the moment the kitchen door was shut.

The koala and the kitten morphed back into Kerek and Zerek. The plastic potty stayed as it was.

"The music stopped," Kerek explained. "We thought you were in trouble. But didn't you see its reaction to the fluffy toys?" he said. "It didn't like them. Much too soft and cuddly!"

"Oh, definitely," said Billy sarcastically. "But I think it was the plastic potty that really terrified the horrible monster from outer space. Well done, Derek!"

"I panicked," said the potty miserably.

Billy filled the kettle, plugged it in and popped a tea bag in a mug. "I just hope she doesn't say anything to Mum and Dad."

"She won't," said Kerek confidently. "Come on, fellow Blobheads. We must return to the High Emperor. Despite the precautions we have already taken, I am not happy leaving him alone."

"Precautions?" said Billy warily. "What precautions?"

"Oh, this and that," said Kerek vaguely. "But let us hope it doesn't come to that – for everyone's sake. Keep Sandra away from the bedroom!"

The two Blobheads waddled away, followed by the plastic potty on its tiny wheels. The kettle came to the boil. As Billy got the milk from the fridge he failed to notice the extended tentacle reaching back into the kitchen from the hall – or the soft *plink* of a purple capsule dropping into the mug.

Chapter Four

Billy arrived in the sitting room with the mug of tea to find Sandra nosing through an album of family snapshots. She looked up.

"So *this* is your baby brother," she said. Billy shuddered. "I really should go up and see that he's all right."

"N . . . no!" said Billy. "He's fine. Sound asleep. You sit down, Sandra. Take the weight off your feet. Drink your tea." He thrust the mug into her hands.

Sandra stared down at the tea. It was only then that Billy saw how strangely the liquid was bubbling. He groaned. The TV, the telephone, the toys – now the tea! Why did the Blobheads always have to interfere? A large purple bubble floated up from the mug towards the ceiling, where it burst. The smell of *Cool Sweat* – only stronger – filled the air.

"I don't think I'll bother," said Sandra. She placed the mug down on the table and strode towards the door. "I'm going to check on that brother of yours."

There was a look in her eyes that Billy didn't like. He had the feeling that Sandra wasn't in a very good mood. If only the Blobheads had just left her alone. She was a babysitter, that was all. A babysitter who happened to be called Sandra. A babysitter who was about to enter the room being guarded by the Blobheads themselves . . .

The word "precautions" flashed inside Billy's head. He had the horrible feeling that if she hadn't liked the fluffy toys or the tea, then she certainly wouldn't be amused by whatever the Blobheads had in store for her upstairs.

And she'd tell his mum and dad.

And he, Billy, would be in serious trouble.

"Sandra," he yelled, dashing after her. "Sandra, wait!"

But Sandra had no intention of waiting. She was already hurrying along the landing. Billy bounded up the stairs after her.

"Sandra!" he shouted again. Her hand was on the doorknob. "Sandra, don't open that door!"

Sandra opened the door.

"Sandra, don't go into the room!"

Sandra went into the room. Billy raced to the bedroom door and froze.

"What the . . ." he muttered.

Inside the bedroom, the air was full of feathers from the pillows; soft, fluffy feathers. Coughing, spluttering and sneezing, Sandra waded through them.

"She's breaking through the feathers!" a voice cried out.

"Who said that?" said Sandra, looking round wildly.

Two fluffy toys and a potty stood in a row between her and Silas's cot.

"Fire!" shouted the silky soft koala, and all three began pelting Sandra with super-fluffy cotton wool balls.

"Ugh! Ouch! Ow! Stop it!" Sandra bellowed as she battled her way through.

"She's still coming!" screeched the cuddly kitten.

"Leave this to me," said the plastic potty. Billy saw a familiar little bottle empty beside it.

"That's Mum's *Heart-Throb* perfume!" he wailed. "It costs a packet."

He lunged forwards. Too late. The potty did a mad wheely and catapulted its smelly contents at Sandra.

"EEEEH-YUK!" Sandra squealed. "That is *disgusting!*"

She grasped her nose, and kept on towards the cot.

"Waaaah! It's still coming!" screamed the kitten. "Hit the foaming nozzles!"

Suddenly, the air was filled with two thick streams of foam as the koala and the kitten squirted shaving cream and styling mousse at her.

With a steely glint of determination in her eyes Sandra skidded over the frothy carpet towards the cot. The fluffy toys were beside themselves. They scurried about, bleeping and buzzing, and flashing purple and red.

The plastic potty snapped at Sandra's heels.

"Go home!" it shrieked.

Billy watched in horror. How on earth could he explain this away? But Sandra ignored the chaos around her. She leant forwards. She reached down into the cot.

"And how are you, little one?" Sandra purred. "Let me tuck you in," she said as she took hold of the corner of the quilt, "and give you a goodnight kiss . . . SILAS!" she screamed.

"Wh . . . what is it?" said Billy, running forwards.

Sandra didn't answer. She simply stared down into the cot, mouth open, eyes wide.

Kevin the hamster sat up on the pillow, his fur all fluffed up. "Cuddle

me if you think you're hard enough!"
he roared.

"Waaaaah!" Sandra screamed.
"WAAAAAH!" And she turned on
her heels and sped from the room.

Billy heard the bathroom door
slamming. The next moment there
was another noise – the unmistakable
sound of a key sliding into a lock. His
parents were back!

Chapter Five

"Sandra?" Mrs Barnes called in a loud whisper. "We're home!"

Sandra emerged from the bathroom. Billy watched her through the crack in the door as she walked along the landing. She had cleaned herself up surprisingly quickly. There was no trace of the foam or feathers or cotton wool balls. She went downstairs.

"I'm going to be for it now," Billy muttered.

Behind him came a voice. It was

Kevin. "A *thank you* would be nice," he complained. "I mean far be it for me to brag, but I have just defeated a horrible monster from outer space."

Billy spun round. He stared at Kevin, in the cot – the cot that should have had his baby brother in it.

"Where's Silas?" he gasped.

The koala, the kitten and the plastic potty morphed back to Kerek, Zerek and Derek once more. Derek tapped his nose knowingly.

"I suggested a less obvious hiding place," boasted Kevin. "There's no end to my talents."

A muffled cooing came from the cupboard. "Silas!" Billy cried, fearing the worst.

He raced across the room and flung the cupboard doors open. Silas looked up and smiled.

"Blobber wobber, Ga-ga, poo-poo,"
he gurgled.

Zerek nodded earnestly. "Wise
words indeed, High Emperor."

Relieved though he was that Silas
was all right, Billy knew he was still in
big trouble. Sandra was bound to tell
his mum and dad everything that had
happened.

"Right, you lot," he told the

Blobheads. "Put Kevin back in his cage, Silas in his cot and clean up this mess." He raced back across the room. "Now!"

As the bedroom filled with feverish activity, Billy pulled the door quietly open and tiptoed onto the landing. He crouched down at the top of the stairs and peeked through the banisters.

"We had a lovely time, thank you," Mrs Barnes was saying. "And you, Sandra? How was your evening?"

Billy held his breath. His heart pounded fit to burst.

"Absolutely fine," said Sandra. "Billy was as good as gold and Silas, well, he's a little angel. Never stirred."

Billy gasped. *Absolutely fine? As good as gold? A little angel?* What was she talking about?

"I am glad," said Mrs Barnes, beaming brightly. She rummaged in her purse. "There," she said, handing over the money. "Do you think you could babysit for us again some time?"

"Oh, yes, please," said Sandra eagerly. "I'd *love* to."

Billy could hardly believe his ears. Was she stark staring bonkers? Or could the Blobheads have done something to her to make her forget what had happened?

As Sandra got ready to leave, Billy slipped back into his bedroom.

As far as he could see, the room was spotless. Silas was asleep again. Kevin was running round and round in his wheel. The three Blobheads were standing, heads together, in the shadows of their sleeping corner.

"How did you do it?" Billy asked them

softly as he climbed into his pyjamas.

"Do what?" said Kerek.

"Make her forget everything?" said Billy.

"We didn't," said Kerek.

"But she didn't tell my parents anything," he said.

"Naturally," said Kerek.

"But—"

"And I bet Sandra also said it would like to babysit again," said Zerek.

"Yes," said Billy. "But—"

"It knows he's here," said Kerek darkly. "And it will be back."

"But next time we'll be ready," said Zerek.

"Give us a month," said Derek, "and we'll make this bedroom so secure the High Emperor will never fall into its evil crutches."

Billy giggled. "It's *clutches*," he said.

"Crutches are—"

"Shhh!" hissed Kerek. "I can hear someone on the stairs."

Billy scrambled into bed and closed his eyes. He heard the door open and his mum and dad creep into the room.

"Don't they look sweet?" said Mrs Barnes.

"Like two little angels," said Mr Barnes.

They kissed their sons and tucked them in, then turned and kissed one another.

"I had such a good time," said Mr Barnes. "We must go out again soon. Just the two of us."

"Very soon," said Mrs Barnes. "Next Saturday. I'll give Sandra a call."

From the shadowy corner of the room came a spluttered gasp and a faint purple glow.

"What was that?" said Mrs Barnes.

Kevin, still whirring round and round in his wheel, let out a sigh of exhaustion.

"Just the hamster," said Mr Barnes. "Come on, let's go and have a nice mug of cocoa."

The moment Mr and Mrs Barnes had left the room, the three Blob-heads emerged from their corner. Flustered, flashing and flapping, they dashed over to Billy's bed and prodded him with their tentacles.

"Billy, get up!" they cried. "You've got to help us."

"What?" said Billy.

"You heard them," said Kerek. "They're going out again next Saturday."

"Which gives us only seven days to prepare everything for Sandra's re-

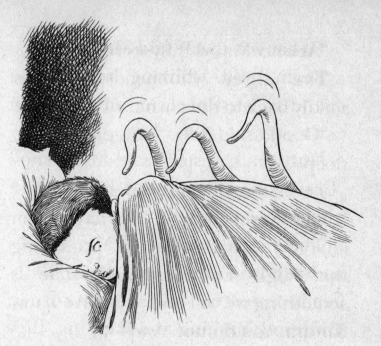

turn," said Zerek.

"Sandra alert!" Derek wailed. "Sandra alert!"

"Come *on*!" said Zerek, and tore back Billy's quilt. "There isn't a moment to lose!"

"NO!" said Billy. He snatched the quilt back. "I've had enough of all this. Go back to your sleeping corner."

"But—" said Kerek.

"At once!" said Billy sternly.

The three Blobheads trooped sulkily back to the corner of the room.

"Good," said Billy. "Now please go to sleep."

There was silence, then, "No, Billy." It was Kerek again. "We have been charged with the duty of protecting the High Emperor, and that is something we will always do. We know Sandra. You do not. And—"

"She's just Mum's secretary's daughter," Billy butted in. "Trying to earn some money. I've been thinking about it. That must be why she didn't tell Mum and Dad about what had happened – because she wants to babysit again, to earn some more money. She's harmless. Completely harmless."

"But—"

"No more! I'm tired. I'm going to sleep." And with that he rolled over and closed his eyes.

"But, Billy," Kerek persisted.

"I'd leave it if I were you," said Kevin the hamster. "You won't get anything out of him when he's in this mood. *I* know."

From outside, the house itself seemed to be falling asleep. One by one, as Mr and Mrs Barnes made their way to bed, the lights went out.

There was someone there, standing in the shadows opposite, watching it happen. It was Sandra. A faint smile played over her thin lips.

When the last light disappeared, she reached up with both hands, seized the hair at the back of her neck and tugged. The wig came away, followed by the mask over her face. Then, with a final flourish, she ripped the entire babysitter suit off and tossed it to the ground.

The moon came out and shone down on a huge, pink monster with twenty-six arms and eight glowing eyes.

"I'll be back!" it cried. "And when I get my hands on the High Emperor I'll take over the universe!" And it threw back its grotesque head and cackled with hideous laughter as it disappeared into the bushes.

"*Ha ha ha haaaa!*"

If you enjoyed BLOBHEADS, look out for

UDDLE EARTH

by Paul Stewart and Chris Riddell

W here would you find a perfumed bog filled with pink stinky hogs and exploding gas frogs? A place that's home to a wizard with only one spell, an ogre who cries a lot and a very sarcastic budgie? Welcome to Muddle Earth. A place where anything can happen – and it usually does.

Joe Jefferson, an ordinary schoolboy from ordinary earth, is about to find his life changed for ever. Prepare for a great battle of good, evil and sort-of OK . . .

A selected list of titles available from Macmillan Children's Books

The Prices shown below are correct at the time of going to press. However, Macmillan Publishers reserve the right to show new retail prices on covers which may differ from those previously advertised.

PAUL STEWART AND CHRIS RIDDELL

Muddle Earth		0 333 94799 1	£12.99
Blobheads		0 330 41353 8	£4.99

SHOCK SHOP

Stealaway	K. M. Peyton	0 330 39739 7	£3.99
Hairy Bill	Susan Price	0 330 93731 6	£3.99
Long Lost	Jan Mark	0 330 39749 4	£3.99
The Bodigulpa	Jenny Nimmo	0 330 39750 8	£3.99
You Have Ghost Mail	Terence Blacker	0 330 96001 7	£9.99
The Beast of Crowsfoot Cottage	Jeanne Willis	0 330 99464 7	£9.99
Goodbye Tommy Blue	Adèle Geras	0 333 99867 7	£9.99
Wicked Chickens	Vivian French	0 333 99462 0	£9.99

All Macmillan titles can be ordered from our website, www.panmacmillan.com or from your local bookshop and are also available by post from:

Bookpost
PO Box 29, Douglas, Isle of Man IM99 1BQ

Credit cards accepted. For details:
Telephone: 01624 836000
Fax: 01624 670923
E-mail: bookshop@enterprise.net
www.bookpost.co.uk

Free postage and packing in the UK.
Overseas customers: add £1 per book (paperback)
and £3 per book (hardback).